Petal Pushers

Coming Up Roses

Read all the Petal Pushers books!

Too Many Blooms

Flower Feud

Best Buds

Coming Up Roses

Petal Pushers

Coming Up Roses

Catherine R. Daly

SCHOLASTIC INC.
New York Toronto London Auckland
Sydney Mexico City New Delhi Hong Kong

To Rebecca and Seamus, my favorite roommates ever.

Special thanks to James Albertelli of Gramercy Park Flower Shop for his generosity, goodwill, and great ideas.

ISBN 978-0-545-21453-7

12 11 10 9 8 7 6 5 4 3 2 1 11 12 13 14 15 16/0

Printed in the U.S.A. 40
First edition, September 2011

Book design by Yaffa Jaskoll

Chapter One

WUWH! I texted my best friend, Becky. I really did wish she was here, sitting next to me in my parents' minivan. Instead, I was sitting next to one of my sisters, Aster, who was listening to her iPod with her eyes closed. Our family was on our way to take our annual fall hike around Lake Winnipesaukee.

ME 2!!! Becky texted right back. IMSB!

I laughed. Of *course* Becky was bored — she was at her six-year-old cousin's birthday party. Can you say "painful"?

SO — WHEN U ASKING HB TO HC? she added.

Seeing those initials made my stomach do an immediate dip, like I had just gone down a big hill on a roller coaster.

HB was Hamilton Baldwin, a boy in my grade. He was supercute and laid-back, with longish, sandy-brown hair, and deep blue eyes. I wouldn't admit it to just anyone, but I had a crush on him. And he had sent me actual text confirmation that he liked me back. No kidding.

Plus, at the end of the summer, he had asked me to go to the movies with him! I had happily accepted. But then my dad lost a filling and had to make an emergency trip to the dentist and I got stuck bringing along my littlest sister, Poppy. Which would have been fine if Poppy hadn't chosen to sit right in between us and I hadn't almost sat down on top of her. And if, during the movie, Poppy hadn't ripped open her bag of M&M's with such gusto that the colorful candies hit everyone in the row in front of us in the back of their heads. But Hamilton was a good sport about it and said he'd had a great time. Still, you couldn't call babysitting your little sister at a movie that featured singing pelicans a date, now could you?

No, you could not. So I figured it was high time Hamilton and I went out on an actual one. HC — Homecoming — was right around the corner. And I had made up my mind to ask him to go with me.

Before I could text back, Becky wrote: GTG & PLAY HOT POTATO — UGH!

TTYL! I typed back. I pocketed my cell phone with a grin and resumed staring out the window. Fall is my favorite time of year. And October is my absolute favorite month, with its sunny days, crisp clean air, and the trees with their brilliantly colored reds, oranges, and golds. The picturesque scenery was an added bonus — covered bridges, fields dotted with pumpkins, grazing horses, and weather-beaten old farmhouses. . . . That's New Hampshire for you.

"Poppy, would you please stop poking me?" Rose whined from the seat behind me. Clearly, none of my younger sisters was as captivated by the scenery as I was.

"No, but thanks for asking," Poppy replied sweetly, as if Rose had just offered her a cucumber sandwich at a fancy tea or something.

I snorted and turned to Poppy. People often said she looked "like a little angel" with her sweet face, chin-length golden ringlets, and rosy cheeks. But she was actually the most stubborn creature you had ever met.

"Mom, make her stop!" Rose said. I was surprised. My

preppy, peppy, blonde sister can generally be counted on to let things roll right off her back. But she looked like she wanted to throttle Poppy right then.

Aster kept her eyes closed and turned up the volume on her iPod. With her dark hair, pale skin, and goth-girl style, Aster has earned Dad's nickname: "my little Wednesday Addams." Though she and Rose are twins, they couldn't be more different.

Mom turned around, a smile stretched tightly across her face. "Poppy, stop poking Rose, please. We're almost there. We're going to have a lot of fun today! By the way, I'm going to need your help on our hike," she added. "Everyone, keep your eyes peeled for beautiful fall leaves on the ground. I have a great idea for the Homecoming bouquets."

Homecoming is a festive reunion weekend at high schools and colleges each fall. At McIlhenny University, which is in my town, there's a football game against Benton, the rival college. There's also a big parade, and the crowning of the Homecoming Queen and King and their court. Granted, the McIlhenny Moose are the absolute worst, with a ten-year losing streak. But just about everyone in town shows up. They all wear antlers and paint their faces red and yellow — the team colors. It's pretty fun, believe it or not.

And Homecoming is a big deal for my family. My dad works at McIlhenny University and my mom is an alumnus. Plus, our family flower store, Petal Pushers, has always provided the arrangements for the Homecoming Queen's float and the bouquets for her and her court.

Rose groaned. "You're putting us to work?"

I leaned forward, interested. "What are you going to do with the leaves?" I asked.

"I'm thinking about bouquets of apricot, orange, and yellow roses, surrounded by fall leaves," Mom replied eagerly.

"Sounds nice," I said. Then I frowned. "But I don't get it. Won't the leaves dry out and turn brown?"

"No!" Mom said triumphantly, beaming. "I have this great idea to dip all the leaves in paraffin to preserve them! They'll last forever!"

I nodded admiringly. "That sounds gorgeous, Mom," I said.

She smiled gratefully at me. "Thanks, Del."

Petal Pushers has been in our family for a hundred

years. Until recently, the store was run by my mom's parents, my gran and gramps. But then they decided to relocate to Florida and left my parents in charge. Things had gotten off to a shaky start. I helped my mom out in the store some afternoons and every Saturday, and we clashed a little: I'm very neat and organized, and Mom, to put it bluntly, is very sloppy. But we'd fallen into a good rhythm, and there was no denying that Mom's creative ideas were pretty amazing.

Also, until recently, Petal Pushers was the only florist in our town of Elwood Falls. But then a new flower shop opened for business. Guess who owns it? None other than Mrs. Baldwin: Hamilton's mother. I know that boy stuff is supposed to be complicated. But I seem to have the special ability to make it even more difficult than usual.

But HB and I had made an agreement to never talk business and not to let it get in the way of our friendship. (He has no interest in flowers whatsoever, so this is way easier for him than me.)

"So are you guys excited to see Nicholas again?" Mom asked as Dad made a turn. "I can't wait to catch up with Debbie. It's been so long!"

I rolled my eyes. Mom had invited her best friend from college, Debbie Tompkins, to come to Homecoming this year. I was kind of bummed that Debbie's son, Nicholas, would be staying with us. Though I hadn't seen him in a couple of years, I remembered him as being a total know-it-all. With super-big ears.

"Actually . . ." Dad said.

We all snickered. The last time Debbie and Nicholas had visited, Nicholas had started nearly every sentence with that word.

Even Mom cracked a smile, which she unsuccessfully tried to hide. "Oh, I'm sure he's outgrown that by now," she said.

I was pretty sure he hadn't, but was in no mood to argue. I steered the subject back on track. "Have you found out what the Homecoming theme is this year?" I asked.

"One of you girls is really going to like this one," Mom replied. "It's 'Coming Up Roses.' Hence, the rose bouquets I'm planning to make."

"Perfect choice," said Rose smugly.

Poppy scowled. "Why not . . . 'Pushing Up Poppies'?" she wanted to know.

All the girls on my mom's side of the family are named after flowers. We've got a Rose, an Aster, a Poppy, a Delphinium (that's me), a Daisy, an Iris, and a Lily. My great-grandma's name was Violet, and *her* mother's name was Hyacinth. I'm not quite sure which is worse, Delphinium or Hyacinth. They're probably equally bad. I prefer to be called Del. Much simpler, as I am sure you'll agree.

Rose shook her head at Poppy. "Because roses are the best flower ever," she said. "Everyone knows that!"

"'One may live without bread, not without roses,'" Dad quoted from behind the wheel. "Jean Richepin." That's what you get for having a dad who's an English professor. A literary quote for every occasion. Whether you want one or not.

"We're here!" Dad said happily as we turned down a narrow, gravelly road and made our way to the parking lot.

As we piled out of the car, Mom tied her bandanna over her wavy, light brown hair — the exact same color as mine — and leaned in to unbuckle Poppy.

Poppy climbed out, yawned, and stretched. Then

she reached inside and grabbed her pink, beaded purse.

I groaned. "Pops, you're not really going hiking with an evening bag, are you?" I asked her.

Poppy gave me a look. "I most certainly am," she replied incredulously. "I never go anywhere without my purse!"

"Don't you mean your *pocketbook*, little girl?" asked Rose. I laughed. My actress sister was doing a spot-on imitation of our great-aunt Lily. Lily is Gran's older sister and co-owns Petal Pushers with Gran and Gramps. Aunt Lily is tough and no-nonsense. But she can be downright mean and controlling. She dresses like an extra in an old-fashioned movie with her tweed suits, seamed stockings, jaunty hats, and yes, fancy pocketbooks. Never "purses" or "handbags."

The worst part? My family loves telling me that I'm just as stubborn and as much of a perfectionist as her. I resent that. A lot.

"Be nice, girls," Mom said as she rolled the minivan door shut behind us.

"Everyone have everything?" Dad asked, then locked the doors. We all smirked at one another. Dad is from

New York and he still hasn't gotten over his compulsion to lock everything tight, even after living in the country all these years.

I reached into my jacket pocket to make sure I had my cell phone. I wasn't sure I'd get service on the hiking trail, but I brought it, just in case. I had also packed a small backpack with a compass, Swiss Army Knife, Band-Aids, aspirin, and extra water. Safety first, that's what my gramps always says. Someone had to be prepared. And in my family, it was almost always me.

I turned to my father just in time to see him polish his binoculars, place his bird-watching book into one of his cargo pants pockets, and tuck his pants into his socks (to avoid ticks). The ultimate geek ensemble. He smiled at all of us. "'Perhaps the truth depends on a walk around the lake,'" he said. "Wallace Stevens."

"Okay, Dad," I said as he adjusted his glasses and — horror of horrors — placed his favorite hat with the earflaps on his head. I swear, he looked just like Elmer Fudd.

Aster elbowed me. "Wabbit season!" she said.

I almost choked. "Duck season!" I shot back. Count on Aster to crack me up with a Bugs Bunny/Daffy Duck routine. She's the quiet one, so when she talks, I always listen because it's usually interesting.

"Very funny, girls," said Dad. "Let's go! Those birds can't watch themselves! Oh, I hope I see a cedar waxwing today," he said hopefully.

Mom gave his shoulder a squeeze. "I hope so, too, honey," she said.

She led the way, holding hands with Poppy. Rose and Aster were right behind them. I came next, and Dad brought up the rear, because he likes to take his time, scanning the trees for birds. We hadn't gone far when Dad tapped my shoulder.

"It's a black-capped chickadee!" he whispered excitedly. "Isn't it beautiful?" He handed me the binoculars and I took a closer look.

Awww. It *was* supercute, with white cheeks and gray wings, darting its little black head around. Even though I wouldn't admit it out loud, I kind of like spotting birds, too. Their movements are very precise, and I like to imagine that they take themselves very seriously.

I handed the binoculars back to Dad and we kept walking, the leaves crunching pleasantly under our hiking boots. I bent down to pick up a leaf of a particularly brilliant shade of red. *This will look great around one of Mom's bouquets,* I thought.

After a while, we stopped for a rest at a spot near the lake's edge. I sat on a rock that jutted up from the shore and stared out at the view. The trees that lined the lake were reflected back in the water, affording us twice the brilliant foliage.

Dad took out his bird-watching book. "We saw three black-capped chickadees, a tufted titmouse, a winter wren, and several cedar waxwings!" he crowed. "Did you hear that? Several!"

I looked at Rose and Aster, who were clearly trying not to crack up. Poppy was busy fiddling with her evening bag.

Mom reached inside her backpack and pulled out a couple of the vibrant fall leaves we had collected. "The colors are amazing," she said. "Who's going to help me dip them when we get back?"

Poppy's hand shot up. "I'll be your assistant!" she cried.

"I'll help, too," I offered. I had never dipped leaves in paraffin before. It sounded like it could be fun.

"Hey," said Dad, stepping back and looking at us all. "Why don't I take a picture of all my girls? We can send it to Gran and Gramps."

Mom's face lit up. "Great idea," she said. She fished around in her backpack but came up empty-handed. "I must have forgotten my camera," she said, looking upset.

"Dad can take it with my cell phone," I assured her. I knew there was a good reason I'd brought it!

I handed the phone to Dad. We all bunched together with the lake in the background, and smiled broadly for Gran and Gramps.

"Nice one!" said Dad.

"I wanna take a picture! I wanna take a picture!" shouted Poppy, rushing up to Dad and trying to grab the phone from his hand.

"Del?" Dad asked.

"Fine!" I said with a wave. "Just show her how."

"I know how to do it," Poppy insisted. She backed up and held the phone up to her face. We smiled again.

"Today would be nice," said Rose.

Poppy adjusted the angle of her shot. "Say cheese!" she said, and snapped our picture. "See, Del, I told you I could do it!" she shouted, waving the cell phone triumphantly. She came rushing toward us.

Mom reached out her arms. "Poppy, be care —" she started to say.

Then, in front of my horrified eyes, Poppy tripped over a rock and crashed to the ground. As she fell, she lost her grip on the phone, which sailed out of her hand.

"Noooooooooo!" I yelled. Almost in slow motion, the phone flipped over, arcing through the air, and finally landed in the lake with a loud *KERPLUNK*.

Chapter Two

"Will someone please pass me the General Tso's chicken?" I asked grumpily.

"Why, certainly," said Poppy immediately, lunging across the table to grab the cardboard container even though it was right next to Dad's elbow.

"Thanks," I said.

But she wouldn't let go of the container. "I'm really really really really really really really really sorry I dropped your phone in the lake, Del," she said sincerely.

Once it had been determined that Poppy was fine — but my phone wasn't — I had gotten pretty upset. And I still hadn't recovered.

I tried to wrest the food out of her hand, but Poppy held it with an iron grip. "Did you forgive me yet?" she asked. When I didn't answer, she pulled out the big guns. "I'll let you take my pink purse to school all day tomorrow. It has three pockets inside."

I laughed, picturing the look on my mortal enemy Ashley's face if I showed up at school clutching a pink, glittery purse with a poodle on it. I'd never hear the end of it.

"Eighth graders use backpacks," I told Poppy.

Despite my annoyance, I relished the sound of that statement. *Eighth grader.* When I had first started middle school I remember thinking that the eighth graders seemed as mature as college students or something. And now I was one of them. I had been for four weeks now.

I realized that my whole family was staring at me, waiting for my reply.

"Fine, Poppy, apology accepted," I said resignedly.

"Yay!" she said, releasing the cardboard container. Then, "Are you going to eat that egg roll?"

Shaking my head, I handed it over to her.

But this situation had not been resolved to my liking yet. My beautiful, bright red phone — with the cute puffy animal stickers I had so carefully applied and the photos I had not yet downloaded to my computer — had sunk to the mucky bottom of the lake, never to be seen again.

I cleared my throat. "Well, what are we going to do about the fact that I am now phone-less? I could be getting important text messages at this very moment!"

Rose snorted. I ignored her.

Dad nodded. "I'll see if Mrs. Kelly can stay a little late after she picks Poppy up from school tomorrow and I'll take you to the mall after my last class," he said. "That work?"

"Sure," I said with a sigh. It had taken me forever to convince my parents that I needed a cell phone in the first place, and now I hated to go even a day without one.

"Is it okay if I have some friends over one day this week after school?" Aster suddenly asked.

"Sure, Rose," replied Mom automatically as she fished around in the foil-lined rib bag.

"That was Aster," I told Mom.

Mom looked up and blinked at the twins. "Oh, of course, Aster," she said. "Sorry." She gave me a quizzical look. I shrugged. If you were going to place a bet on which twin was going to invite friends over after school, the odds were that it was going to be outgoing Rose. Not silent, spooky-poetry-writing Aster.

"So what day do you want to invite them over?" Mom asked Aster, still looking surprised.

"How about Wednesday?" Dad asked. "My last class gets out early that day."

"Sounds good," said Aster.

Mom turned to Rose. "Do you want to have some friends over, too?" she asked.

"No thanks," Rose mumbled, staring down at her half-eaten plate of General Tso's chicken. She looked up to see us all staring at her. "I'm busy preparing for the play try-outs," she said defensively. "If I want to get a lead role, I can't waste time hanging out with friends! This is middle school now. Serious stuff."

I still hadn't gotten used to the fact that my twin sisters went to the same school that I did. Every once in a while, if I passed one of them in the hallway, I'd have a brief moment of confusion — two worlds getting mixed up, like your grandma showing up in gym class. But it was starting to feel less weird as time went on.

After dinner, I went to Dad's office to call Becky.

"Are you calling me from a *landline*?" she asked in disbelief.

"I am," I said. "Poppy dropped my cell phone in Lake Winnipesaukee."

Becky burst into laughter. "Sorry," she said. "But you have to admit that is pretty funny."

"It will be funny eventually," I told her. "Just not yet."

"So what's going on?" Becky asked. "You calling to get HB's number so you can ask him to HC?"

I laughed. Our texting shorthand had started to overtake our conversations, too.

"No, I think this requires an in-person invitation," I explained.

"Very brave!" Becky said. "But it's not like he's going to say no."

"You never know," I said, feeling a swell of nervousness. "This whole thing is freaking me out a little."

"It's pretty obvious he likes you," Becky said. "You don't bring birthday cakes to girls you don't like. It gives them the wrong impression."

"I guess . . ." I said. Over the summer, Hamilton had

hand-delivered me a birthday cake. Strawberry shortcake, my absolute favorite. "But that was way back in July," I argued. "People change their minds. Or he could have other plans. Or maybe he doesn't like football," I finished lamely.

There was a moment of silence. "Or maybe you've never asked anyone out before," Becky said wisely.

"Yeah, maybe I haven't." I smiled. My best friend knew me pretty well.

"You can do it," she said. "Piece of cake. So when are you getting your phone?"

"Tomorrow after school," I said. "Thank goodness."

"Did you keep a list of all your numbers?"

Oh no. I felt embarrassed by my lack of organization. It so wasn't like me! "I meant to, but I never did," I confessed. "Can you give me the ones you have? I'll have to input them all over again. How annoying."

"Sure," she said, and gave me our mutual friends' numbers. "And just in case you chicken out and decide to text him instead, here's Hamilton's," she said.

As I was copying down the numbers on a sheet of paper, someone picked up the other line.

"I'm on the phone!" I said crossly.

"Oh, sorry, Del," Aster said. "Let me know when you're off."

I had gotten so used to my cell, I had totally forgotten about the lack of privacy on landlines.

"Rose?" asked Becky.

"It was Aster," I told her. "Calling her new friends!"

"Weird!" said Becky.

"Del, we're about to dip the leaves!" Mom yelled from the kitchen.

"You can be the assistant's assistant!" shouted Poppy.

"I should go. I'll see you tomorrow," I told Becky.

In the kitchen, I found Poppy standing on a stool as she and Mom intently watched a block of paraffin melt in the double boiler. Every surface was covered with flattened paper grocery bags. As soon as the paraffin had completely melted, we took turns holding leaves by their stems and dipping them in the thick, clear liquid, laying them on the paper bags to dry. The leaves looked even more vibrant with their shiny wax coating. When we were done, the kitchen was bursting with preserved leaves of every shape and color.

Mom sighed contentedly. "Gorgeous, girls, just gorgeous," she said.

Dipping the leaves had taken my mind off everything. But as I headed upstairs, I could feel my stomach do a flip-flop of nervousness. I couldn't believe I had decided to ask Hamilton on a date the next day. Now that I had told Becky, it was definitely real.

But he could out-and-out say no. He could laugh at me. I could have food stuck in my teeth (it has happened before!). I could trip and fall. What if I burped or accidentally spit on him?

I decided to get ready for bed before my imagination totally ran away with me. I washed my face, brushed my teeth, and put on a cozy pair of pajamas. I got under my comforter and read a chapter of an old favorite, *Caddie Woodlawn*. Before I shut off the lamp on my nightstand I automatically reached for my phone to check for texts. Then I remembered. Bummer.

"Let's go!" I called up the stairs for the third time that morning. I was waiting, not so patiently, for my sisters so we could walk to school together. They were never ready. It ate into my hanging-out-with-my-friends-in-the-morning time. And this morning, I was in desperate need of some moral support before I asked Hamilton out. The very thought made me feel sick to my stomach.

"Jeez, Del," said Rose as she slowly walked down the stairs, still brushing her blonde hair. "No need to freak out. There's plenty of time." She rolled her eyes. "Only you would be in a big rush to get to *school*."

Aster ran down the stairs with an apologetic look, her dark hair falling into her eyes. I smiled, despite myself, at the sight of the twins side by side.

Rose was wearing pink-and-white-striped leggings, a denim miniskirt, and a pink hoodie with cute mitten-shaped pockets. Aster, on the other hand, was wearing black jeans, black boots, and a shapeless black pullover sweater that must have once belonged to Dad. The only hint of color was the red T-shirt that showed through the moth holes in the sweater.

I looked down at my own outfit — skinny jeans, green suede flats, and a green-and-purple flannel shirt. A very nice asking-a-boy-out-for-the-first-time outfit, if I did say so myself. If I actually managed to ask Hamilton out, that was. Otherwise, it would be a very cute losing-your-nerve ensemble.

The three of us set off for school at a snail's pace. Rose was really dragging her feet today.

"How do you like middle school so far?" I asked them.

"Fine," said Rose tersely.

"Not bad," said Aster.

"Are your classes interesting?" I asked.

"Sure," said Rose.

"I like English the best," said Aster. "We're reading 'The Legend of Sleepy Hollow'!"

"Cool," I said.

"Bo-ring," said Rose.

"You have Mr. Packer, right?" I asked.

Aster nodded.

"Try to stay out of the first two rows if you can," I advised her. "He's a crazy spitter!"

"Tell me about it!" said Aster with a laugh.

She and I chatted the rest of the way about her upcoming report on Washington Irving. Rose lagged behind, kicking at pebbles in her path. English never was her favorite subject, I remembered.

We walked up the granite steps to the school. As I pushed open the heavy wooden door, I asked Aster and Rose if they wanted to join me in the cafeteria. It seemed like the sisterly thing to do, but secretly, I hoped they wouldn't say yes. I had important, private things to discuss with my friends.

Aster said she had friends to meet in the library, and Rose said she had some homework to finish, so I headed to the lunchroom alone.

"I heard about your phone!" was how my friend Jessica Wu greeted me as I approached the table. "That's terrible!"

"I know," I said as I sat down across from her. Spiky-haired, skinny, and slightly spacey, Jess looked cute as ever in a cropped sweater, miniskirt, and tights.

Sitting next to Jess was Heather Hanson, who looks like a china doll with her blonde curls and blue eyes, but happens to be very tough. To my left was Amy Arthur, with her red hair and funky, rectangular glasses. Amy totally worships her big sister, Amber, who's in high school.

Amy is also the most trustworthy person I've ever met. And next to Amy sat Becky, with her flawless dark skin, warm brown eyes, and gorgeous, curly black hair. I smiled at her. I was lucky to have a BFF who was smart, sweet, funny, and always put a positive spin on things.

"I'm going to get a new phone after school today," I told them.

"Thank God," said Jessica.

"No wonder you didn't return my call yesterday!" Heather squealed. "I was feeling insulted until Becky filled me in." Then her eyes widened with horror. "What if Hamilton tried to call you and thinks you're ignoring him?"

"Shhhh!" I said, taking a quick glance around the cafeteria.

"Don't worry," Heather told me. "He's on the breakfast line. He can't hear us."

I shook my head. Heather is completely boy crazy and keeps tabs on not just her crushes, but everyone else's.

I took a deep breath and told my friends about my plan to ask Hamilton to Homecoming today.

"Do it!" Heather squealed very loudly.

"So how do your really feel?" I asked, wincing. Too late, I remembered why I usually tend to keep things, as Gramps would say, close to the vest (except around Becky, of course). Now my friends would never let this rest until Hamilton and I were sharing a hot dog in the bleachers at the football game.

Amy nodded. "Totally a great idea," she said. "And I'm glad you're going to do it in person. Much better than texting or calling. Trust me, I know about this stuff from Amber."

I gulped, wishing I felt as confident. Texting Hamilton would be so much easier. . . .

"Look at that," Amy said disgustedly. I followed her gaze. Ashley Edwards, my arch-nemesis, and her two interchangeable best friends, Sabrina and Rachel, had just entered the cafeteria. They were pointing and laughing at a seventh grader on crutches who was struggling to carry a heavy tray. I shook my head.

Sometimes I couldn't believe that Ashley and I had actually once been best friends. Okay, it was way back in preschool. And we had parted ways over a Halloween costume. Yes, I said Halloween costume.

Sure we'd had a brief friendly encounter over the summer after I had saved her birthday party from certain disaster. But when school started in September, we were back to being mortal enemies. It was like our positive moment never even happened.

"I can't believe they're not helping him!" Amy sputtered, standing up. "I'll show them how human beings are supposed to act!"

"No worries," said Heather. "Da-da-da-da," she sang. "It's Super Hamilton to the rescue!"

I spun around in my seat. And there was Hamilton, putting down his books and food on a nearby table. He talked to the struggling seventh grader, took the tray from him, and walked with him to an empty table. Once Crutch Boy was settled, he thanked Hamilton, who waved it off and walked back to get his breakfast.

Heather batted her long eyelashes at me. "Your hero!" she said. I made a face at her, but I could feel my cheeks getting very warm.

"Oh!" Jessica said, wide-eyed. "Is *that* the guy you want to ask to Homecoming?"

Becky rolled her eyes. "Oh, Jess!" she said lovingly.

"Shhhhhhhh!" Amy and Heather hissed at Jess.

"That's him," I told Jess softly.

Suddenly, Heather kicked me under the table. Hard.

"Oww, what's up with that, Heather?' I asked, bending down to rub my shin. When I straightened up, I saw that all my friends were staring at something behind me.

"Huh?" I said, turning around to see what was so interesting. And there he was. Super Hamilton himself, balancing a hot chocolate and a buttered bagel on a stack of books.

"Hey, Del," he said. "How have you been?"

"Great," I replied.

"Gym isn't the same without you," he added.

"I know," I said. "I mean, for me, either. It's weird. I mean it's still fun, well, not when we play stupid games like Steal the Bacon — remember when we had to play that game? That wasn't fun at all, at least I didn't think so, but maybe you . . ."

Another kick under the table. I managed not to yelp, but I did give Heather a dirty look.

This was not going well. My face was hot again and my mind was a total blank. I glanced over at Becky for encouragement. She was looking at me with extra-large eyes, nodding her head. I knew exactly what she was trying to tell me. *Ask him to Homecoming.* The rest of my friends were all smiling at me encouragingly.

Hamilton shifted his weight. "All right, then," he said. "I guess I'd better find a seat and eat my breakfast before —"

Suddenly, I found myself standing up. And talking. "Hamilton, I wanted to ask you a question . . ." I started to say, ignoring the intense flip-flopping that was going on in my stomach.

"Hey, Hamilton!" a sugary voice called out then. I groaned. I knew that fake cheerful tone anywhere. It was Ashley. She sauntered up to us and looked me up and down, taking in my outfit with a sneer. Despite myself, I felt my heart sink. It stung a little that my carefully chosen outfit did not meet the fashion queen's approval.

"Hello, Delphinium," she said icily.

"Hey, Ashley," said Hamilton. "What's up?"

"Oh, I have a question about the Spanish homework, but it can wait a minute," she said. "Del, why don't you ask Hamilton *your* question first?" She looked at me with a mocking smile on her face. "I can wait."

Gulp.

"Um, it wasn't a big deal. I'll ask you another time," I mumbled to Hamilton.

"Are you sure?" asked Hamilton kindly.

I sank back down into my seat. "Yeah, I'm sure," I said. I watched dejectedly as Hamilton and Ashley walked off together.

"Foiled again," I said ruefully.

"There's still time," Becky said gently. "Don't worry, Del, you'll get up the nerve."

"I don't know about that," said Heather. I told you, she's tough.

It wasn't too long before the bell rang for class. I said good-bye to my friends and headed to history. Halfway down the hall, I spotted Aster, walking with four other girls, all dressed in black. They were giggling together. *Have the twins switched bodies?* I wondered.

"Hey, Aster," I said. I smiled at her friends.

"Is *that* your sister?" one of the girls squealed. "Isn't she an *eighth grader*?"

I grinned to myself. It shouldn't have been such a thrill to be looked up to by the sixth graders.

But somehow it was.

Chapter Three

After school, my sisters practically had to run to keep up with me on the way home. I was in a huge rush to get my new phone. My dad would be stopping by the house on his way from the university to pick me up and take me to the mall.

While Aster and Rose went inside, joining Poppy and her babysitter, Mrs. Kelly, I anxiously waited outside for Dad. Had he gotten held up with a student? Got called into a departmental meeting? Completely forgotten about our shopping trip?

But to my great relief, his car soon pulled up. I raced over to the sidewalk and yanked open the passenger-side door.

"'Adopt the pace of nature,'" said Dad, "'her secret is patience.' Ralph Waldo Emerson."

"Whatever, Dad," I told him with a grin. I snapped my seat belt on, feeling giddy with anticipation. Sure, I was eager to get my new phone, but I was also kind of looking forward to spending some time alone with my dad. With three little sisters, we didn't get to hang out too much, just the two of us.

"Everyone at the university is really excited about Homecoming," Dad said as he signaled and pulled away from the curb. "They say the parade is going to be bigger than ever this year."

"Do they also say that the McIlhenny Moose are finally going to win a game?" I asked him, smiling.

He laughed. "No, they certainly aren't saying that yet," he said.

I pictured myself in a cute outfit, cheering (you've got to be optimistic) at the game with Hamilton by my side. *Yeah, as soon as you ask him!* I reminded myself. After that morning's debacle, I had briefly considered dropping a note into his locker, but Amy had talked me out of it. She'd convinced me that in person was the only way to go.

"So what kind of phone should I get?" I asked Dad, pushing thoughts of Hamilton aside for the moment.

"How about one with a camera?" he suggested in all seriousness.

"Dad, they *all* have cameras these days," I told him. "Remember? That was how I lost my phone in the first place."

"Oh, that's true," Dad said absentmindedly. "My phone doesn't have one, though!"

Dad pulled into the mall and parked the car. I took note of the section. My family has been known to forget where they parked — much more than once. One time, Mom had to wait until the mall closed and most of the other drivers had taken off before she found our van. True story.

Just my luck, we had parked near the entrance that forced us to walk right past Fleur — the flower shop owned by Hamilton's mom. My stomach sank.

"Hey," said Dad when he saw the gleaming windows. There were spotlights focusing dramatically on three floral arrangements which, frankly, looked a little busy to me. "That's the competition, isn't it?"

"Yes," I muttered, taking his hand and trying to pull him past.

But Dad paused to peer inside. His eyes lit up as he saw the shiny metal counters and the gleaming flower fridge. "Wow," he said. "Very modern. Should we go in and check them out?"

"No way!" I yelped. Dad gave me a quizzical look.

"I mean, we wouldn't want them to think we were spying on them or anything," I said quickly.

Dad didn't know this, and hopefully never would, but I *had* actually spied on Fleur. Not once, but twice. I didn't want to take any chances that Hamilton's mom would recognize me. Or, even worse, that Hamilton would be there and introduce me to his mom, who would *then* recognize me as Secret Agent Bloom.

This seemed to make sense to Dad, and thankfully, we went directly to the phone store.

Grown-ups are always complaining about the DMV, but I think phone stores are the most painfully slow places ever. I put my name down on a list and browsed through all the fancy phones I couldn't have, until my name was called. Luckily, it was time for an upgrade for me and I picked out my new phone (pink, cute, flip, decent camera). Our salesperson, Missy, who wore bright red lipstick and had long, jet-black hair, activated the phone. She was about to ring us up when she noticed something on her computer screen.

"Can I see your phone?" she asked Dad. He fished into his pocket and handed it to her.

"Whoa! Look at this!" she called to her coworker. "When's the last time you saw a phone this humongous?" They both laughed out loud. "You haven't had an upgrade since you bought this dinosaur!" Missy told Dad. "Are you ready for a new phone?" She peered at his phone from under her bangs. "Who knows how long the duct tape is going to keep that battery in place?"

Dad shrugged, but then allowed himself to be led over to the display of smart phones. And before I knew what was happening, he was the proud owner of a brand-new iPhone. I looked down at *my* new phone and frowned. It didn't look quite so fun or sleek anymore.

With a shrug, I turned on my phone. Two seconds later, it started ringing! I cringed — it was one of those embarrassing ringtones that the phone came programmed with. I'd have to play around with it and fix that right away.

The number calling was one I didn't recognize. Who could it be? My heart skipped a beat. What if it was Hamilton?

I flipped it open. "Hello?" I said uncertainly.

"Hey, Del," said Mom. "I guess you got your new phone."

I felt a weird combination of disappointment and relief.

"I did!" I said. "And you're never going to believe it — Dad got one, too!"

"I guess that's why my call didn't go through to him," Mom said. "That's good. That old one was as big as a walkie-talkie. Listen, can you guys pick up some dinner tonight? I'm going to stay a little late at the store to work on the Homecoming bouquets. Mrs. Kelly will stay with the girls until you and Dad get home."

"Munchbox?" I suggested hopefully.

"Sounds good to me. Don't forget to order extra drumsticks. I hate when you girls fight over them."

"Sure," I said, hanging up. "That's crazy," I told Dad. "That was Mom calling from Petal Pushers. I didn't even recognize the number."

"That happens to everyone," said Missy. "Nobody knows anyone else's numbers anymore. We're all used to speed dial."

Dad laughed. "I still remember my best friend's number from grammar school," he said. "Five-five-five-three-eight-two-three!"

"Impressive, Dad," I said, rolling my eyes. I was glad I'd gotten all my friends' numbers from Becky and had copied them into my binder.

"When I was a kid we had rotary phones," Dad explained to Missy. "None of this pressing a button. If you missed one number, you had to start dialing all over again. If there were a lot of nines or zeros it could take forever!"

Missy looked puzzled. "What's a rotary phone?" she wanted to know.

Dad sighed. "Man, I feel old," he said.

As we walked out of the store, Dad immediately began worrying. "I think I spent too much on my phone.

I don't need all these special things. Maybe I should return it."

"But now you can check your e-mail from anywhere," I explained. "It will be really helpful for work. Plus, there are all these cool apps you can download. . . ."

"Apps?" he said, looking confused.

I gave him a look. Did he live in a cave or what?

"You know, games and stuff," I explained.

"Oh, I don't need any of those things," he said. "Aren't they just for kids?"

"No way! You can get online dictionaries and Bartlett's Quotations!" I told him.

He brightened. "Oh, that could be fun. I guess I'll read the manual and see what it's capable of." He thought for a minute. "Hey, I know it's almost dinnertime, but you want to split a soft pretzel?"

"Of course!" I said. You didn't need to ask me twice if I wanted my favorite mall snack of all time. We headed toward the food court, which was pretty empty. Dad sat at a table and pulled out his phone and the manual. I knew he would read it cover to cover. The man loves reading so much he would read anything he could get his hands on.

I got in line behind a tall, blonde woman at the pretzel stand, who was talking on her cell phone. Her voice sounded familiar. I was reaching into my pocket for my money when I overheard something that gave me pause.

"That's right," the woman said. "I need five hundred sixteen-inch red rose stems and two hundred yellow ranunculus. They need to be here by next Friday, the latest."

Tall. Blonde hair. Ordering flowers. Was I standing right behind Hamilton's mom? As she paid for her pretzel and coffee, I stole a quick look at her profile. Yup. I'd recognize her anywhere.

Luckily, she didn't notice me. When I got back to the table with the warm, buttery pretzel, Dad was fully fixated on his new phone.

"I just downloaded this game," he told me excitedly. "And it's free! It's called Gnomeland! Look at all those cute little guys! They all have different-colored hats, and they each have a different power. This guy in the purple hat is the musical gnome. He plays his glockenspiel and it helps the beans grow. And I get points when I harvest the beans so I can buy things!"

I gave him a look. Was he for real? "Gnome things?" I said.

Dad nodded excitedly. "Yes! Like hoes and shovels and tractors and stuff like that!"

"Sounds fascinating, Dad," I said sarcastically.

But apparently it was. He was so preoccupied with the game that I got to eat the whole pretzel myself. No complaints there. And then he stayed in the car and played when I went into the Munchbox (owned by my classmate Eleni Nikolopoulos's family) for fried chicken and all the trimmings. Eleni was there doing homework in a booth, so we hung out for a bit while I waited for my order.

"Tell me more about Trollville," I said to Dad when I got back into the car with the food.

"Gnomeland, silly," he corrected me. I settled back into the passenger seat as he told me about all of the different types of beans you could plant and harvest. It sounded crazy lame to me. But Dad was enthralled.

❁ ❁ ❁

MENU. SELECT. ADDRESS BOOK. SELECT. ADD NEW CONTACT. ENTER FIRST NAME. ENTER LAST NAME. ENTER NUMBER.

Over and over and over. I was sitting at the kitchen table after dinner inputting all my friends' numbers from my binder. I accidentally put in Jessica's number incorrectly and had to start over. This was so boring. But now my phone had a ringtone that sounded like a frog croaking, which made me very happy.

Mom pushed open the kitchen door, a scrap of paper in her hand. She had a big smile on her face. "I was just IMing with Debbie," she said excitedly. "She gave me Nicholas's number to give to you. He's totally excited about spending time with you on the trip and he has a couple of questions. Maybe you could give him a call."

I squinted up at her. "Mom, are you kidding? Questions about *what*?"

She handed me the scrap of paper with Nicholas's number on it. "Oh, who knows. Maybe he wants to know if he should bring his Atari," she said cluelessly.

"Fine, Mom," I said. "I'll call him." I put in his number, Amy's, and a couple of other kids from school as Mom hovered next to me. I blushed like mad as I input Hamilton's number. Luckily, Mom didn't notice.

She smiled. "It means so much to Debbie and me that you and Nicholas are going to spend some more time together," she said.

"How much time?" I asked warily.

"Well, they'll be here for almost a week," Mom explained. "I think you guys will strike up a nice friendship!"

I realized there was no arguing with her. Why do adults think that just because they're friends with someone, you are automatically going to be best buds with their friend's kid? I mean, it wasn't *that* long ago that she was my age, you know?

I said good night to my mom and headed upstairs to finish my homework. I passed by Poppy's room and could hear her jumping on her bed, saying, "I'll brush my teeth tomorrow instead, Dad. I swear. I'll shake on it!"

I walked into my room, sat down at my neat desk, and smiled. The pens and pencils were carefully arranged in a

McIlhenny University mug. My laptop was gleaming, my textbooks in a perfect pile. Ah, order.

I opened up my laptop. I had a couple of questions due tomorrow on the cotton mills of New Hampshire, but first I decided to check my e-mail. Nothing much — some spam that I immediately deleted, and from Heather, a link to a YouTube video of a funny cat who liked to sit in boxes of all sizes. I made a mental note to show it to Poppy the next day. She'd love it.

Suddenly, a message popped up in the corner of my computer.

Hey, Del, it's Nicholas! it read.

Oh boy, I thought.

Hey, Nicholas! I typed in unenthusiastically.

I didn't get a call from you, so I decided to IM.

Sheesh, give a girl a minute!

Totally psyched about our visit, he continued.

Me too, I typed. Good thing the sarcastic tone in my head didn't translate on IM.

Homecoming should be a lot of fun, Nicholas wrote.

Yeah . . . just to warn you, our team is not exactly . . . I started to write.

But he beat me to it. *Though I hear that the McIlhenny Moose have quite a record! Haven't won a game in ten years!*

I smiled ruefully. He had done his research.

Actually, I have a couple questions about my upcoming visit, he wrote. *You have a minute?*

Sure.

Where will I be sleeping?

In the garage, I wanted to write, just to see what he would say.

Guest room, I wrote.

Queen bed or twin?

I had to think about that one for a minute. *Full,* I wrote. Then I added, just because, *actually.*

Should I bring my own pillow?

IDK, we have plenty here.

Hmm . . . maybe I'll bring mine. Hypoallergenic.

I had no reply to that one.

Do you have wireless?

Of course.

I don't want to brag, he wrote, *but I'm a bit of an amateur photographer.*

He was thirteen years old, so I doubted he'd be a professional. But I let it go.

Nice! I typed.

I'm looking forward to taking some shots of the foliage, and also some action shots at the football game.

Sounds good! I wrote.

Just wondering — is there anything at McIlhenny that's one of a kind that would be fun to photograph?

I was stumped. *The statue of Sarah Josepha Hale?* I thought. *The Dairy Queen where Elvis Presley allegedly ate three Peanut Buster Parfaits?* Then I remembered a random piece of information that Dad had shared with me on my last visit to the university. I was sure this was something that Nicholas wouldn't be able to be an expert on. With a smile I typed: *You're in luck! McIlhenny Library has a new exhibit on Tupperware!*

Silence. I grinned. I had stumped him!

That's right! he wrote back. *Earl Silas Tupper was from New Hampshire!*

Sheesh, is there anything this kid doesn't know? I wondered.

Del, you made my day! he wrote. *Believe it or not, I love Tupperware.*

Oh, I believe it, I thought. One thing was for sure. Nicholas was still a totally dorktastic know-it-all.

Ugh. I could hardly wait for his visit to be over and he hadn't even arrived yet.

Chapter Four

"Hello, Hamilton, would you be interested in accompanying me to the Homecoming game?" I asked my reflection in the bathroom mirror.

No, too formal.

I tried again.

"Hey, Hamilton, want to go to the big game next weekend? With me?"

"Why, certainly, Delphinium," I replied in a deep, didn't-sound-very-much-like-Hamilton-at-all voice.

"Hey, Del," a voice said from behind me.

I spun around, mortified. Then I breathed a sigh of relief. It was just Poppy.

"What are you pretending?" she asked. "Can I play, too?"

"I . . . um . . ."

Luckily, Mom called up the stairs at that moment. "Girls! Breakfast!"

"How about later, Pops?" I told her.

She shrugged. "Okay," she said and took off.

I turned back to the mirror for one last glance and frowned at my reflection. I took off the pink scarf I had looped around my neck. *Too Ashleyish,* I decided.

My entire family was already at the breakfast table by the time I got downstairs.

"So what shall we plant this morning, Poppy?" Dad asked.

The rest of us had thought Gnomeland was cute enough, but Poppy had shown a real interest. "It reminds me of Snow White and the Seven Dwarfs," she'd said. "That's a movie I saw when I was a little girl." That made us all laugh, because she had seen it just two weeks before.

"Lima beans!" she told Dad now.

"Those take six hours to grow," Dad replied. He frowned and checked his watch. "I'll be between classes. Perfect! I can harvest them then."

"Yay!" said Poppy, clapping her hands.

Rose, Aster, and I exchanged glances. Seriously, this gnome stuff was getting out of hand.

Mom piled Dad's plate with scrambled eggs and placed a kiss on top of his head. "You're so funny," she told him. "I love seeing you and Poppy having so much fun together."

"I got this game for you girls," Dad told all of us.

"Gee, thanks," said Aster drily.

I laughed, looking at my dad hunched over his phone, letting his eggs get cold. "I can tell."

After the usual waiting period, I headed to school with my sisters. I was relieved that Rose and Aster were listening to music together on Aster's iPod so I didn't have to talk at all. My thoughts kept returning to Hamilton, and whether he would say yes when I asked him to Homecoming. *If* I asked him.

But I couldn't ask him if I couldn't find him. I searched high and low for Hamilton. Waited at his locker until I got too embarrassed and left. Scanned the cafeteria for him at breakfast.

At lunch, I sat down at the table and unwrapped my ham and cheese on rye (with mustard) unenthusiastically.

"I can't find Hamilton anywhere," I told my friends. "Weird, huh?"

Heather made a face. "Oh, I forgot to tell you. Hamilton wasn't in math class this morning. It's kind of gross. Rumor is he has . . . conjunctivitis."

Pink eye? I thought.

"Oh my gosh!" said Jessica. "Is he going to be okay?"

"I would think so," said Amy.

"But won't they need to take it out?" Jess asked.

We all stared at her. *Huh?*

"Take out his eye?" I finally asked.

"No, silly," she said. "His — you know —" She pointed to her stomach.

Complete silence. Finally, Becky said, keeping as straight a face as she could, "Not *appendicitis*, Jess, *conjunctivitis*."

At her blank stare, Becky explained, "Pink eye."

"Ewwwwwww," we all said.

Pink eye had been making the rounds of Sarah Josepha Hale Middle School for weeks. It was an uncomfortable infection that brought itchy, watery, pink eyes. Hamilton would be out for a couple of days waiting for the antibiotics to clear it up. I felt relieved for my reprieve, sorry about Hamilton's itchy eyeballs, and a little grossed out, too. Not a stellar combination.

That afternoon, I trudged home alone. Rose was at auditions for the play. Aster was, shockingly enough, going to the mall with her new friends. Poppy was at a playdate, and Dad had office hours. I decided to head to Petal Pushers to see how things were coming along.

I paused to look inside the front window of our cozy little store. Mom's latest window display was a fun fall combination of cheerful yellow and red zinnias; Chinese lanterns with their orange, papery seedpods; and these fluffy, white flowers called bunny tails. Inside, I saw Mom, a goofy little smile on her face as she finished up a simple yet stunning arrangement of orange orchids. It made me smile, too. The woman totally loved flowers. Just like me.

I pushed open the door, relishing the cheery jingle the bell made. I took a deep, appreciative sniff. The air smelled like it always did: sweet and slightly spicy.

"Well, if this isn't a pleasant surprise!" Mom said, tucking a strand of hair behind her ear. "How was your day?"

"All right," I said. "You need any help?"

Mom glanced around. "Not really," she said. "We can go home together as soon as I clean up."

I felt a little disappointed. I had been hoping to help out with an arrangement. "Maybe I'll go in the back and start my homework," I said.

I headed to the back office, and gasped. Clearly, I hadn't been here in a while.

Mom, left to her own devices, had left her mark — with a vengeance. Overflowing files, half-opened desk drawers with papers spilling out. A cold cup of coffee with a ring of mold sat on the desk next to a petrified half-eaten bagel. What a disaster.

I opened a cupboard, pulled out a garbage bag, and snapped it open. Homework would have to wait.

I tied up old newspapers and catalogs for recycling (or "Being Good to the Earth," as Poppy called it). I Pledged the old wooden desk, enjoying the lemony scent. Then I began to tackle the desk drawers. Mom has a terrible habit of shoving mail that doesn't look urgent or interesting into them, to get to at a later date. Many times, the later date never comes. "Junk mail. Junk mail, junk mail. Junk . . . Hey, wait a minute," I said. The return address read

BOSTON BEANS, a popular chain of coffee shops. They served expensive coffee drinks and decent baked goods. You either loved them for their convenience or hated them because they were almost everywhere. I myself really liked their fancy hot chocolate, which you could get with both whipped cream *and* marshmallows. I tore open the envelope, hoping to find some coupons.

But there weren't any coupons inside, just a piece of expensive-looking stationery. I unfolded the letter and began to read. I shook my head. That couldn't be right. *I must have read that incorrectly,* I thought. I began reading the letter again. A chill ran through me and I literally shuddered. I stood up, still feeling discombobulated, as if I had just had a scary dream but wasn't sure if I was awake or still asleep.

Slowly, I walked to the front of the store.

"Hey, Del!" Mom called, a wilted rose in each hand. "Almost ready to go?"

I opened my mouth but nothing came out. "I . . . I . . ."

Mom dropped the roses on the counter and came up to me, putting her hand on my arm. "Del, what's wrong?"

she asked worriedly. "You look like you've just seen a ghost."

"I was cleaning," I finally managed to say.

Mom laughed. "I know it's a mess, but don't you think you're overreacting a bit?"

"I found this," I said, holding out the letter. "It's from Boston Beans."

"Oh, that," she said. "Coupons, right? I should have just thrown that away. Their coffee is so bitter."

I shook my head and finally found my voice. "That's not it. Boston Beans wants to open a store in Elwood Falls," I told her. "And I'll give you three guesses as to where they think the perfect location is."

"Boston Beans?" said Dad that night at dinner. "That's preposterous! We have the Corner Café. We don't need a Boston Beans on Fairfield Street!"

I nodded in agreement. "Unfortunately, they think that Petal Pushers is the perfect spot for their new store," I told my family, who all wore expressions of shock. "And they're willing to pay a lot of money for it."

"How much?" asked Dad.

Mom named a sum so large that everyone at the table gasped. Dad even put down his iPhone, mid–cannellini bean harvest.

"Daddy, they're going to wither!" Poppy squealed. She scooped the phone up and began to harvest the beans. The sound effects were comical. *Ploop, ploop, ploop, ploop, ploop.* Too bad I couldn't laugh.

"The crops are saved," Poppy said solemnly.

"That's a lot of money," Dad said to Mom thoughtfully. "Think about it. We could open a bigger place. Hire a full-time delivery person. Maybe another designer to work on arrangements."

I stared at him in disbelief.

"And not have to worry so much about every little thing," he added. "We'd have a cushion."

Mom wrung her hands. "That's all true," she said. "But it's our *place.* It's been in the family for a hundred years!"

"I know," said Dad, "I know. But we have to at least consider it."

Mom's eyes brimmed with tears.

I put down my fork. "You can't be serious!" I said to my father. "We can't sell the store!"

I thought about the uneven floors and the drafty windows. The rattling flower cooler and the scratched wooden worktable that was a century old. Those things might sound like good reasons to sell the place, to some people. But I loved everything just the way it was. With the name change that we had introduced when Mom and Dad took over *and* a new location, there would be nothing left of the original place. Nothing left of Gran and Gramps. It left a hollow feeling in the pit of my stomach.

Rose shrugged. "The place *is* kind of old," she offered. "We could get a cool, new store."

I glared at her. "Like Fleur? That place is cold and impersonal. It's the history of our store that makes us special. The old-fashionedness of it. The tradition."

Mom sighed and dabbed her eyes with her ever-present bandanna. This one was red. I could feel a tightness in the back of my throat and my eyes filled with tears, too. I blinked them back. I hate to cry in front of people, even my family.

Aster spoke up. "And Boston Beans is a chain! I thought we didn't like chain stores. They put the mom-and-pops out of business and all that."

Like our store, I thought, but then shook my head. They wouldn't be putting us out of business. Just forcing us to move!

"That does bother me," Dad said thoughtfully. "Contributing to the decline of Main Street."

Now *that's* what I was talking about.

"But they're offering an awful lot of money," Rose pointed out.

Dad nodded. "It's true."

Mom blew her nose.

Dad leaned forward. "I know this is hard," he said in measured tones. "But this is a business. We need to discuss this with Gran and Gramps and Aunt Lily. The decision is ultimately up to them, since they are the owners."

Mom nodded grimly. "You're right," she said. "I'll call them now."

I hid my smile. There was no way Gran and Gramps would agree to this ridiculous idea. Petal Pushers would stay where it belonged. No question about it. We'd be telling Boston Beans to get lost in no time.

❀ ❀ ❀

"Well, of course we have to sell," said Aunt Lily. "I'll have my lawyer contact Boston Beans tomorrow morning. End of story."

It was an hour later. Aunt Lily, upon hearing the news from Mom, had insisted she come over immediately so we could call Gran and Gramps together.

"Whoa there, Lily," said Gramps. "This is a family decision."

We were all huddled around the computer in Dad's office, staring at Gran and Gramps on the screen. As always, I marveled over how happy and relaxed they looked. Life in Key West was treating them well. And they loved their new place. I had been relieved to hear they were renting it instead of buying. It gave me a small hope that maybe one day they would return to Elwood Falls.

"I don't understand why you all aren't jumping at this chance," Aunt Lily said huffily. "Offers like this don't come along every day."

I cleared my throat. "What do *you* think, Gran and Gramps?" I asked pointedly.

Gran looked at Gramps. "I don't want to speak for both of us, but I think that the choice needs to be made by those we left in charge — Daisy, Ben, and Lily. You know how things are going right now."

"I agree," said Gramps. "So really think this through. Decide what will be best for business and for everyone."

I sighed. Gran and Gramps were being totally reasonable, like they always were. It was just so frustrating. They owned two-thirds of the business and could have told us all what to do and we would have had to listen. But no, they had to go and be fair!

Gramps laughed. "I see that look, Del!" he said. "I can't be a dictator. It just isn't right, especially with us being far away. You are going to have to make the decision for yourselves."

I looked over at Aunt Lily. It was abundantly clear that her mind was set.

But then again, so was mine.

Chapter Five

I had managed to keep my worrisome news to myself all day at school, under the ridiculous theory that maybe if I didn't talk about it, it would just go away. But on the walk home together after Yearbook Committee, Becky asked the seemingly innocent question, "Everything all right, Del?" and the story came spilling out of me like water from an open fire hydrant.

Becky shook her head. "Wow, that's quite the conundrum!" she said.

I smiled despite myself. Becky liked to use new words as much as I did.

"It isn't a conundrum for me," I said. "I know what the right thing to do is."

"But there are a lot of people involved in the decision," Becky explained. "And it *is* a lot of money to turn down."

"You can't put a price on tradition," I told her. I liked the sound of that and decided to file it away for our next family meeting.

Becky gave me a thoughtful look. "Del. I know how much you love the store and how much it means to you. But a business is about making money, you can't forget that."

I scowled. Just whose side was Becky on, anyway?

"But I understand how you feel," she added. "Honestly. I want you to keep the old store, too. I can't imagine your family anywhere else!"

That was more like it. I smiled at her and put my hands deep in my pockets. "It's just . . . the store feels like my home, you know? When I was little I used to beg my parents to take me there instead of the playground. Before Gran and Gramps left, it was my refuge from my crazy family."

Becky nodded. "So what's going to happen next?"

"Aunt Lily is insisting that we start checking out available spaces for the store to relocate to."

"Well, maybe she'll find this amazing space that you like even better," Becky suggested.

I stared at her.

She shrugged. "You never know," she said. "Stranger things have happened."

Becky was the ultimate the glass-is-half-full person and, in her case, it was usually half full of something incredible, like strawberry lemonade.

"Don't you ever get tired of looking at the bright side of things?" I asked her.

She grinned and shook her head. "Nope."

I sighed. "Well, I guess we just wait and see what happens," I said, getting that hollow, empty feeling in the pit of my stomach.

When I got home, I was looking forward to some peace and quiet. But I was at home — so what was I thinking? Immediately, I tripped over several pairs of black Doc Marten boots haphazardly discarded by the front door. Then I remembered that Aster was having some friends over that afternoon.

I couldn't help myself. I lined up everyone's shoes and placed my own in my usual spot. I was about to head upstairs to my room when I heard Poppy's voice.

"Awesome!" she cried. I wandered into Dad's office to find him and Poppy playing that stupid game. Again.

"Del, we just got six snozzleberries!" Poppy shouted.

"Um . . . great," I said.

"We've moved up to a brand-new level," Dad told me. "These snozzleberries are going to open up a whole host of opportunities! Nine more and we can get a Gnome wishing well!"

"I'm really excited for you both," I said sarcastically. They didn't even seem to notice.

I went to the kitchen to grab a predinner snack. Aster and her friends had completely taken over the rough wooden table, which was littered with opened bags of chips and pretzels, notebooks, and library books. The girls had been chattering loudly, but when I walked in, silence fell over the room.

"Working on your Washington Irving report?" I asked my sister, grabbing a bottle of lemon-lime seltzer from the fridge. "Hi, I'm Del," I added pointedly.

"Oh, sorry!" Aster said. "These are my friends Maureen, Ellen, Susan, and Monica."

I waved and smiled at them all. They were all wearing black, just like Aster. Monica had purple streaks in her blonde hair. Ellen was wearing a black cardigan with huge holes where the elbows should have been. Maureen had safety pins in her ears, and Susan was wearing black lipstick. Aster was fitting right in, that was for sure.

They all stared back at me. "Hey," said one. Ellen, I think. Or maybe it was Maureen.

"So you guys stole all the snacks?" I teased them.

Susan got up and handed me a bag of Smartfood. "It's all yours," she said. "Frankly, I prefer Pirate's Booty."

Aster laughed and threw a piece of it at Susan, who expertly caught it in her mouth.

I stared at my sister. Had a playful alien taken over her body or something? This was so unlike her!

I tucked the bag of white cheddar popcorn under my arm and headed out of the kitchen. Then I heard the front door slam shut. I spun around. There stood Rose, looking decidedly unhappy.

"All those ugly boots!" she scoffed. "I guess the goth girls are still here?"

"Yeah," I said. "They're in the kitchen."

Rose made a face.

"Actually, they seem pretty nice. . . ."

Rose dropped her backpack to the ground and roughly

removed her jacket. She let it fall to the floor. I was just about to say something, then thought better of it. "That's because they worship eighth graders," she said meanly.

"You should be happy that Aster is making friends," I scolded her. "It's about time, you know."

"Whatev," said Rose.

I was all set to protest, but then thought better of that, too. "Um, bad day?" I asked her as she marched past me and started up the stairs.

"Don't even get me started," she replied.

I tentatively followed behind her.

"Anything you want to talk about?" I asked when we got to the landing. Rose marched to the bedroom that she and Aster shared (it was decorated pink on Rose's side, black on Aster's) and closed the door in my face.

Guess not.

When Mom got home and started dinner, I went downstairs to set the table. The last of Aster's new friends was putting on her battered Docs.

"Good-bye, Del," Safety-pin Girl said as she slung her backpack over her shoulder and headed out the door. She had lots of holes in her black tights.

"Good-bye . . . you!" I called after her.

"That was Maureen," Aster said, shaking her head.

I headed into the kitchen. Mom had already set the table, and in the middle was a sample Homecoming bouquet that she had brought home. The tightly packed apricot, orange, and yellow roses were surrounded by the border of paraffined leaves. She had also added a little sprig of acorns. The ring of shiny leaves perfectly complemented the gorgeous fall hues of the roses.

"It's gorgeous," I told her truthfully.

"Thanks, Del," Mom said as she picked up the pan and expertly flipped the chicken stir-fry. "I think I finally got it right."

Everyone filed in for dinner. Dad speared a bean and held it up for all to see. "String beans!" he said. "We haven't planted any of those yet, Poppy. They only take two hours to grow. We can harvest before bedtime. What do you think?"

"Certainly!" said Poppy. "String beans it is!"

"I have a new rule," said Mom. "No Fairytown at the dinner table!"

"Gnomeland!" Poppy and Dad said at the same time.

I glanced over at Rose. She wasn't eating, just pushing stir-fry around on her plate.

Mom sighed. "All right, Rose, you've got to tell us what's wrong," she said.

"Something's wrong, Rose?" asked Dad. Classic absent-minded professor.

Rose started to say something, then stopped. She dropped her head and mumbled into her shirt.

"What?" we said in unison.

"I didn't get the part I wanted," she said.

"Oh, honey," said Mom, putting down her glass and rubbing Rose's arm. "That must be so disappointing. But you have to remind yourself . . ."

"That I'm only a sixth grader," Rose finished sullenly. "There are no small parts, only small actors. I've already heard it from the director. It doesn't help."

Poppy leaned forward. "There are small actors in your play? Like gnomes?"

Rose ignored that.

"So who are you going to be?" Dad asked.

Rose knit her eyebrows together. "Townsperson number four. I say, 'It's a lovely day for a hayride.'" She laughed ruefully. "I hope I can remember my *line*. Del, can you help me practice my *line*?"

I winced. There wasn't much to say to that.

"Sorry, Rose," said Aster.

"May I be excused?" Rose asked.

Mom looked at Dad, then nodded.

After she left, we all sat in silence. Even though it had been a long shot that a sixth grader would have gotten a big part, it still had to be tough on Rose. She was used to being the star of the show.

Mom changed the subject. "You know, I still haven't heard a word about Homecoming," she said. "Can you see what's going on with Laurie Rice?" she asked Dad. "I left her a message days ago and I haven't heard back. I can't wait to tell her about the ideas I have!"

Laurie Rice was a philosophy professor at the university, and she was also the head of the Homecoming Committee. She was the person who made the decisions about the flowers. I knew Laurie would be floored by Mom's bouquets. How couldn't she be?

"Oh, that's right," said Dad, slapping his forehead. "I totally forgot. Laurie's on sabbatical this term."

I felt a twinge of worry. A sabbatical is time away for a professor to do research or write a book. Laurie was clearly not going to be picking the Homecoming flowers this year.

"Oh dear," said Mom, putting down her fork. "So who's in charge?"

Dad patted her arm. "I'll find out tomorrow, sweetie, I promise," he said.

Mom nodded, but her forehead was creased with concern.

Dad pointed to the bouquet. "Your design is amazing. Whoever is in charge this year is going to be sure to love it!"

Since Rose was off sulking, I helped Aster rinse the plates and stack them in the dishwasher. Then I started on the pots and pans.

The house phone rang. I reached out a soapy hand and picked it up. "Bloom residence," I said.

"Hello, may I please speak to Daisy Bloom?" a woman's voice asked.

"May I ask who's calling?" I said, looking pointedly at Aster and Poppy, who, along with Rose, were lacking in phone etiquette skills. They simultaneously stuck out their tongues at me. Nice.

"This is Marcia Lewis," the voice said. "From the Homecoming Committee."

A big grin spread over my face. I brought the phone to Mom, who was curled up on the living room couch knitting Aster a long black scarf.

"It's a woman named Marcia Lewis," I whispered. "She's from the Homecoming Committee."

Mom sat up straight and put her knitting to the side. I handed her the phone, then lingered in the entryway to listen.

"Hello, this is Daisy Bloom," she said. "Hi, Marcia, how are you? Oh, that was so nice of Laurie to ask you to call me. Thank you. I can't wait to show you our amazing idea for the Homecoming bouquets, I was hoping we could set up an appointment this week. . . ." She paused to listen and a frown crossed her face. "Oh, I see. Well, is that your final decision?" She paused. "Okay, well, thank you for your time. Good-bye."

Mom sat there, hanging her head. I was too afraid to

say anything. Dad did it for me. "Oh, Daisy," he said sympathetically. "That didn't sound like it went so well."

"It certainly didn't," Mom said with a groan. "This Marcia person told me that she already hired another florist to do the bouquets!"

My heart sank. "Fleur," I said. I felt sick to my stomach. It all made perfect sense. On Monday, at the mall, I had overheard Hamilton's mom ordering a huge quantity of red roses and yellow ranunculus — McIlhenny University's school colors. I should have seen this coming.

Mom nodded grimly. "Fleur," she confirmed.

Dad frowned. "Marcia is the new geography professor. She just started this fall. She probably doesn't know that Petal Pushers has always done the flowers for Homecoming. Do you think I should talk to her?"

Mom shook her head no emphatically. "She's allowed to make her own decisions," she said. But then she dropped her head into her hands. "But she didn't even give us a chance. This is the first time that our family isn't doing the Homecoming bouquets in almost ninety years. How am I going to tell Gran and Gramps?"

My head started spinning as the true significance of what had just happened sunk in. No Homecoming business meant we would be behind in our budgeted sales for this month. We had been counting on that money. I put my hand to my forehead. This would give Aunt Lily yet another reason to insist we needed to sell the store.

What I didn't want to think about was that maybe she was right.

As I lay in bed that night, my phone pinged, which meant I had a new text message. I reached over and picked it up. It was from Heather.

RUMOR IS HB WILL B BACK 2MRW! GONNA ASK HIM 2 HC???????

I shut off my phone and flopped over to my side.

With this new turn of events, I didn't know *what* I was going to do about Hamilton. Fleur had stolen away our business, yet again.

Hamilton and I had agreed not to let business get in the way. But it didn't seem possible, not this time.

Chapter Six

"What are we going to do with all these leaves?" Mom asked sadly, holding a bright red-and-orange maple leaf by the stem.

I had stopped by the store after school and found her contemplating the collection of paraffined leaves, which she had spread out over the counter.

"I guess you could use them in birthday bouquets," I told her with a shrug.

I wished I could be more upbeat. But school had been bleak. Hamilton was back, his eyes not looking pink in the least. Or at least that's how it looked from far away. I was keeping my distance, too upset about the turn of Homecoming events to be friendly.

At least I was spared from discussing the store,

Homecoming, or Hamilton in the cafeteria. Becky had warned my friends that all of those subjects were off-limits. That was a relief.

"I don't know," Mom said, setting the leaf down. "I just wish there was something really special I could do with them." She sighed. "Not as special as Homecoming bouquets for the whole town to see, but something."

"Well, just be sure to use them before Thanksgiving," I said. "After that, everyone's going to want nothing but Christmas and Hanukkah colors."

"You're right," said Mom. "You're always so practical."

I felt terrible. Not just for Mom, but for all of us. Petal Pushers had been a part of the Homecoming tradition since the college was first founded in 1925. It seemed crazy that our involvement was over, just like that.

"You're never going to guess who came to the store first thing this morning," Mom said, walking behind the counter.

I was pretty sure I could guess. "Not . . ."

Mom nodded. "Aunt Lily. She marched in here, set her

pocketbook down on the counter, and said, 'So I heard you lost the Homecoming business.'"

"But how . . ." I started. I shook my head.

"Old Lady Mafia!" we said together.

Mom and I have this theory. There seems to be a secret society of old ladies in Elwood Falls who pass around bad news seemingly as soon as it happens. It's like they have gossip radar or something. These ladies rarely have cell phones or even know how to use computers, so it's a wonder to me how they disperse news so quickly.

"So now she has even more ammunition to convince everyone we need to sell," I said sadly.

Mom nodded. "She said that Fleur is going to continue taking away our business unless we take a new approach. She wants Dad to start looking at new spaces with her. This Saturday."

I looked around the store, a lump forming in my throat. The place was so sweet and homey, from the creak of the wooden floorboards to the chipping paint on the walls. It was just so *comfortable*, like a cozy bathrobe or slippers. It was my favorite place in the world. And there was a really good chance I could be losing it.

It was finally Friday. Another nice thing about being an eighth grader (besides the adulation of the younger students) is the extra free period you get. Luckily, Amy had a free period at the same time, so we had met at the library to catch up on homework and hang out.

We sat at a table in the corner, Amy cramming for a science test. I was all caught up on my schoolwork, so I was inputting the phone numbers I had accumulated all week.

Amy looked up from her notes. "I know I'm not supposed to mention his name, but um, you-know-who is at the checkout counter," she said softly. "He must have the same free period as us."

I looked up to see Hamilton and Mike Hurley checking out two big stacks of books.

"And I also think he saw you," Amy warned me. "Not that I'm mentioning his name or anything," she added.

Without even thinking, I stood up and darted up the stairs to the balcony.

I had a bird's-eye view of the entire library. I could see Carmine Belloni and Penelope Peterson passing each other notes and giggling. I spotted Bob Zimmer, the school bully, drawing an anchor tattoo on his arm in ballpoint pen. I stifled a laugh. Who did he think he was, Popeye the Sailor Man? And then I saw Hamilton and Mike heading right over to my table. They chatted with Amy for a bit. I guess one of them asked her a question because I saw her shrug in response. After what seemed like forever, the boys finally left the library.

When the coast was clear, I came back down the stairs.

Amy's face was bright red. "Oh my God. I made such an idiot out of myself!" she whispered. "I meant to say 'How are you guys?' but I was thinking about his conjunctivitis, so I ended up saying, 'How are your eyes?' instead. Like he wants to be reminded about his pink eye! And then when I tried to explain, it just made it worse. How embarrassing."

"I bet he laughed it off," I said wistfully.

"He did," she agreed. She looked at me searchingly. "Del, he's a really nice guy, you know."

"I know," I said sadly. He was. That's why I liked him in the first place. (Plus, there were those piercing blue eyes. . . .) But it was just too complicated for me. And at this point, I wasn't even sure I wanted to go to Homecoming anymore, anyway. Maybe I'd just admire the Tupperware with Nicholas instead.

"How many appointments do you have with the realtor today?" Mom asked Dad on Saturday morning as we headed out to the store. Rose, Aster, and Poppy were coming, too.

I bent to tie my right, pink shoelace. I had an orange one in my left sneaker. A small gesture, but it cheered me up a little.

Dad looked up from his bean harvest and smiled. "Four," he said.

"Ask a lot of questions," I told Dad as I stood up. This whole thing was giving me a major headache.

"I will," he said, already returning to his game.

"We planted pinto beans this morning!" Poppy reminded him as we walked out the door. "They'll be ready to harvest at three o'clock. Don't let them wither! We need those snozzleberries!"

As soon as we got to the store, I put Rose and Aster to work dusting and sweeping. Poppy insisted on cleaning the front windows, but after she knocked down the display, crushing some of the Chinese lanterns and spilling water everywhere, I set her up at a worktable. She looked as happy as a clam to be surrounded with a pile of past-their-prime flowers we were going to throw out anyway and some curling ribbon. She immediately opened her purse and began hauling out doll accessories — brushes and barrettes and boots and sparkly minidresses. I gave a little laugh. Poppy could fit an awful lot of stuff into one tiny evening bag.

As Mom organized the orders for the day, I walked up to her. "You know I am entirely against selling this place," I said.

Mom put a cool hand to my cheek. "Of course I do," she said. "I feel the same way. But what can we do? Aunt Lily is so set on it."

"I've been thinking. Aunt Lily said that to compete with Fleur we would need to take a new approach," I said. "But who's to say it needs to be as drastic as selling our store? Maybe we could take a new approach . . . to Homecoming."

Mom frowned. "I don't see what we could do. The flowers for the float and bouquets have already gone to Fleur. What's left for us? The queen and her court can't carry two bouquets each. We can't *both* decorate the float."

I frowned. "Dad said this parade was going to be bigger than ever. Maybe we can do a new float, like . . ." I frantically tried to think of something. "Like . . . a moose made out of roses. Now wouldn't that be fun?"

Mom almost choked on her coffee. "Do you know how long it would take to design and make something like that? Weeks! Homecoming is next Saturday!"

I frowned. "All right. But there's got to be *something*," I said. I brightened. "How about wreaths of roses for the queen and her court to wear in their hair?"

Rose spoke up from across the room. "Brill idea, Del,"

she said sarcastically. "No self-respecting queen is giving up that sparkly tiara."

"She's right," Mom said. "Though there's no need to be rude about it," she added pointedly to my sister. She put her hand on my shoulder. "Look, Del, I want to be a part of Homecoming, too, but there's nothing we can do."

Dejected, I leaned on the counter next to Poppy.

"Play with me, Del," she begged. I can never resist Poppy's puppy-dog eyes

"Sure," I said. "For a minute. What are we playing?"

"Dress store," Poppy told me. She picked up her Barbie doll and walked it up to me. "Hello, madame," she said. "May I come into your store? I need a fashionable party dress to wear to the ball."

I stifled a laugh. Poppy's doll, as Gran would say, was in her birthday suit. "Ah," I said. "I see you are unexpectedly naked and in need of some clothing. Well, you have come to the right place. Welcome to my fashionable party-dress store. May I interest you in an evening gown, perhaps?" I picked up a tiny, satiny purple dress.

"That would be lovely," Poppy said.

I struggled to get Barbie's rigid arms into the slinky dress. Poppy looked at the outfit and frowned. "Too purple-ish," she decided. "It needs to be fancier." I fished a little white feather boa out of the pile and draped it around Barbie's neck. Poppy shook her head. Still not fancy enough. Then she had a sudden inspiration. She hopped off the stool, ran to the tape dispenser, and brought it over. When she had climbed back up to her perch, she started removing rose petals from one of the flowers and taping them to the skirt of the dress.

"Cute, Pops," I said absentmindedly. She continued to add layer after layer of sweet-smelling rose petals to the skirt.

"Voilà!" Poppy said. "Presenting the Flowery Rose Skirt!" She hopped Barbie up and down. "Do you like my fashion?" she asked me seriously.

I didn't answer. The wheels in my brain began to turn. A rose-petal dress — would it be possible?

I grabbed Poppy by the hand and we walked over to Mom, who was flipping through the day's orders.

"Look at what Poppy made," I told her.

Mom glanced up. "So pretty, Poppy," she murmured.

"No, Mom, really look. What do you think?"

Mom looked from the Barbie to me, then back again. "You want me to make a skirt entirely out of rose petals for the Homecoming Queen?" she said in disbelief.

"No," I said.

"Well, that's a relief," Mom replied.

"I want you to make a dress entirely out of *rosebuds* for the Homecoming Queen," I explained.

"What?" Mom gasped.

"Sounds weird," said Rose.

"I don't know," said Aster slowly. "It could be cool."

"It was *my* idea," Poppy put in.

I patted her on the head. "Yes, it was. Thank you, Pops," I said.

I grabbed Mom's notebook and turned to a clean page. I quickly sketched a long evening gown, then started to draw in rosebuds.

"I just can't figure out how to attach them," I said.

Mom thought for a minute, her forehead wrinkling. And just when I was sure she was going to say "impossible!" she grinned. She reached into the cooler and pulled out a deep-red rose, flipped it over, and studied the base.

"I think this could work! I would sew them on," she said. "Glue gunning them would make it too stiff and heavy." She nodded. "Sewing is the way to go."

"So we're going to try this crazy idea?" I said, my spirits lifting.

Mom nodded. "Let's do it right now!" she said. "I'll take care of arrangements that need to go out today and you girls run home and get the stuff we're going to need." She paused, and I grabbed a piece of paper to take notes. "I'll need my sewing basket, and a dress to practice on . . ." Mom thought for a minute. "I have a strapless dress in the back of my closet we can use. Someone spilled a glass of red wine on it at a wedding and I've been meaning to dye it black. It will be perfect for this project!"

"Anything else?" I asked her.

Mom nodded. "Big needles. Waxed thread. And my dress form. I'm going to need to adjust the dress a bit." She looked at my sisters and me. "What are you waiting for? Go! Go! Go! We have a dress of roses to make!"

Chapter Seven

As soon as we got home, I sent Rose up to the attic to get the dress form. The rest of us gathered the other supplies. After I located Mom's dress shears in the cutlery drawer (don't ask), I went upstairs to see if Rose needed help.

"Rose?" I called into the shadowy attic.

"Over here," she said. I found her sitting on the floor. She looked up, a smudge of dust on her cheek. She was sifting through a box marked ROSE'S PLAY PROGRAMS. "Remember when I was Annie?" she said wistfully. She started to sing. "The sun will come out . . ."

"I remember," I said, cutting her off. Rose had adored being the little redheaded orphan and had remained in character throughout the whole production. There had been far too many "gee whiskers!" and "leapin' lizards" for my taste. Plus, she had insisted on calling our dog, Buster, "Sandy," which totally confused him.

But Rose looked so sad I couldn't say anything to her about wasting time. So I tried distraction. I saw a weird headband that kind of looked like Martian antennae with sparkly red hearts on top and put it on to make her smile. Then I helped her put the scrapbooks away and finally, behind a large, wire birdcage in a dark corner, we located the dress form. It loomed in the darkness, ghostly white and headless.

"Kind of spooky," said Rose.

As we left the house, Poppy held the sewing basket on her arm like she was Little Red Riding Hood, off to visit her sick grandmother. Aster was carrying the dress and a bag of chocolate-chip cookies we had found in the kitchen. Rose and I carried the dress form — she held the base and I had my arms wrapped around the shoulders. We were quite an odd sight.

We giggled self-consciously as we made our way to the store. We got a lot of curious looks and one woman even slowed down her car and pointed us out to her kid in a car seat in the back. Finally, we reached Fairfield Street.

"Oops. We forgot one thing!" I said, backtracking half a block to Nellie's Notions on Pine Street.

I sent Aster and Poppy inside for the big sewing needles and a couple of spools of the waxed thread that Mom had requested. Rose and I stood outside with the dress form, feeling slightly ridiculous. As a joke, I threw my arm around the form's shoulders.

"Well, isn't this a cute picture," said a voice.

I groaned.

Ashley Edwards always seemed to show up at the most embarrassing times. It was a special gift she had.

She stood on the sidewalk in front of us with her two matching best friends.

"Del, this must be your new friend," Ashley said snarkily, pointing to the headless form.

To my surprise, Rose laughed. I gave her a dirty look.

"Hello," I said. I decided to be polite. "This is my sister Rose."

"Oh, I know Rose," said Ashley, waving her hand. "I see her at school all the time."

I frowned. I had no idea Ashley knew who my sister was.

"So, rumor has it Petal Pushers isn't doing the Homecoming flowers," Ashley said. "I was really sorry to hear that."

I gave her a look. She was sorry? I highly doubted that.

"Well, we've got to run," she said. "Oh, and Del?"

"Yes?" I said.

"Nice headgear." She and her friends laughed and laughed as they took off down the street.

My heart sank. Surely I didn't still have . . . I reached up. Sure enough, the stupid antennae headband was still on. I snatched it off.

I gave Rose the evil eye. "It didn't cross your mind to tell me I still had this stupid thing on my head?'

She shrugged. "I thought you knew."

When Poppy and Aster emerged from the store, Poppy grabbed the headband out of my hand and put it on her head. "It's about time you shared!" she said.

Inside Petal Pushers, Mom squealed when she saw Poppy. "My Deely Boppers!" she cried. "I haven't seen those things in years!" My eyes widened. Mom wore those things in public — on purpose?

Miraculously, Mom had finished all of the orders that needed to go out. She was ready to devote the rest of the day to making the rose dress. She had laid out every red rose we had in the store on the worktable. But first things first. She reached into the sewing basket and pulled out the tape measure.

"Del, I think you should model the dress," she said. "I'll have to adjust it a bit to fit you."

"Lucky stiff!" said Poppy. Rose scowled. And I have to say, I was pleased to be picked.

Mom took my measurements and adjusted the dress form accordingly. Then she ripped open some seams on the dress and pinned it to fit the Del-sized form.

Meanwhile, we cut the roses under Mom's strict instructions — precisely one-quarter of an inch under the sepals, which are the pointy green things on the bottom side of roses. They protect the flower when it's a bud.

When that was done, I went into the bathroom and slipped on the dress, which fit almost perfectly. We didn't have a full-length mirror, but I wondered if I looked as glamorous as I felt in the strapless dress, red wine stain or not. I stepped back into the shop and spun around, the skirt poofing out prettily.

"Looks great," said Mom.

"Give it a rest, Maria von Trapp," Rose said grumpily.

With a sigh I went back into the bathroom and changed back into my regular outfit. I came back out with the dress and Mom laid it on the counter.

She ran her finger over the stain on front of the dress. "Let's start with the top," she said. "See how it goes."

We all leaned forward in anticipation. Even Rose's bad mood seemed to have lifted in the excitement.

Mom threaded a needle, picked up the first rose, and, with a certain amount of effort, forced the needle through the stem just below the sepal.

"Ouch," she said. "Where's my thimble?" I rooted around in the sewing basket until I found it. Then she sewed the rose right to the dress. All alone like that, it looked like a lame corsage someone had mistakenly pinned to their belly button. But as Mom added more roses, the dress suddenly began to take form.

We were surprised to discover how many roses it took to cover just the top half of the dress. We had seriously underestimated how many roses we would need.

"Well, good thing we're not in a rush," I said.

"Um . . . we kind of are," said Mom. "I already called Marcia and set up an appointment for this afternoon."

I laughed. "Yeah, right," I said.

"I'm not joking," Mom said.

My mouth fell open in shock. "Mom! You set up an appointment with her before the dress was even made?"

Mom shrugged. "I'm thinking positively," she said.

I shook my head, but I couldn't argue.

We tried calling Dad to help us, but we couldn't reach him. I hoped it wasn't because he was too busy viewing the perfect new location for Petal Pushers!

So I sent out the 9-1-1 text to my friends. HELP! WE NEED 4 DOZ RED ROSES ASAP! CAN YOU BRING TO PP? PAY U BACK, PROMISE!

It's in times of need that you find out who your friends are. Mine all passed with flying colors.

B RIGHT THERE! texted Becky.

C U SOON! wrote Jess.

HA! I'M AT MALL. CARE IF THEY COME FROM FLEUR? wrote Heather.

That made me laugh. NOPE! I wrote back to her.

Help was on the way!

So we had quite an audience as Mom sewed the final rose onto the top half of the dress.

"It's gorgeous!" Becky squealed.

"Awesome!" cried Jessica.

"I want one!" said Heather.

Now all we had to do was convince Marcia Lewis that she wanted one, too.

We closed the shop and my friends took off. We dropped the protesting Rose, Aster, and Poppy at Mrs. Kelly's, and practically flew to the university. When we got there, I crouched in the back of the van and put on the dress.

Soon, Mom and I sat in Marcia's office, waiting for her to arrive. My heart beat double-time as I adjusted the large black shawl that covered the top half of the dress.

Finally, Marcia entered her office. She was a little older than my mom, with jet-black hair pulled into a long, sleek ponytail. She was dressed casually but stylishly, wearing jeans, a black turtleneck, and knee-high black boots.

"Marcia," said Mom, standing up and reaching out her hand. "Thank you so much for agreeing to see us on such short notice."

"This had better knock my socks off," Marcia said brusquely. "Do you have any idea how busy I am? It's a week before Homecoming!" She sat behind her desk and crossed her arms. "You've got . . ." She checked her watch. "Seven minutes. Start talking."

I was glad Mom was in charge. I was so nervous I was pretty sure I'd be unable to form a complete sentence.

Mom took a deep breath. "Well, since this is your first year as Homecoming director, we realized you probably wanted to do something that would really make people sit up and take notice. So we created a floral piece that is guaranteed to get everyone's attention."

"We have all the flowers we need," Marcia told her. But despite herself, she looked intrigued. "So where are these showstopping flowers?"

Mom nudged my leg. I stood and positioned myself next to Marcia's desk, the shawl still wrapped loosely around my shoulders.

"Any Homecoming Queen can carry a bouquet of flowers," Mom said. "But how many Homecoming Queens get to *wear* an entire dress made of flowers?"

That was my cue. I dropped the shawl to the floor dramatically and did my best supermodel pose.

"Oh my," said Marcia.

"Imagine if you will," Mom said, "a ball gown made entirely of roses from head to toe. Everything will truly be coming up roses!"

Marcia looked stunned. I watched her carefully. Was that good or bad? Then she picked up her phone. "The Homecoming Committee has got to see this," she said, dialing a number. "Alison," she said into the phone, "can you drop everything and round up the committee?"

Mom and I exchanged a hopeful glance.

About ten minutes later, the room was filled with faculty and students.

The room was buzzing as everyone gathered around me to take a closer look. "It's amazing!" someone said. "Beautiful!" said another.

This time, Mom and I exchanged excited glances. The dress was a hit!

There was a knock on the door. A very pretty student with long, straight, dark hair and dark eyes popped her head in. "Oh, Professor, I'm sorry, I didn't realize . . ." she said when she took in the crowd of people jammed into Marcia's office. Then she saw the dress. She stared at it, her eyes as round as saucers.

"This is Emily, one of our Homecoming finalists," Marcia explained. "So what do you think?"

"Oh. My. God," Emily said. "If I don't get to be Homecoming Queen and wear that dress I am just going to die."

Mom and I grinned at each other. *Yes!*

Marcia nodded. "Okay. We'll need to discuss it and take a look at our budget and get back to you," she said, shaking my hand and then my mother's. "Thanks so much for coming in."

My face fell. I thought we would get our answer today.

Mom and I walked through the familiar campus in silence. We passed by the quad on the way, filled with students acting like it was a warm spring day: eating lunch, tossing Frisbees, playing guitar. I stared at one guy who was walking around barefoot.

"There's one on every campus," said Mom.

"Well, everyone really seemed to love the dress!" I said. "I'm sure we'll be hearing from Marcia soon with good news."

Mom shrugged. "They did like it. A lot," she said. "And a 'we'll see' is definitely better than a 'no.' But they might not have the budget for it. A dress made entirely of roses is not going to exactly be cheap, you know."

"I know," I said. The wind gusted, swirling dead leaves around our feet. I pulled the shawl around me more tightly.

"We should have brought your clothes with us," said Mom worriedly. "You're going to catch your death of cold."

I smiled at her Gran-ism. "I'm fine, Mom," I told her.

As soon as we reached the parking lot, Mom stopped in her tracks. "Delly? Do you happen to remember exactly where I parked the van?" she asked, looking around the parking lot. I groaned. I had been distracted and anxious when we arrived and hadn't made my usual mental note.

She cupped her hand over her eyes and squinted. "Oh, there it is!" she said, relieved. We headed over to the white van. I walked over to the passenger side and jerked open the door. I blinked. Something wasn't quite right.

Mom looked at the air freshener that hung from the rearview mirror. "Vanillaroma," she read. "Where did *that* come from?"

"Mom," I said, looking at the floor mats, which were decidedly unfamiliar. "This isn't our car."

Laughing sheepishly, we slammed the doors shut.

"You know what Dad would say," I told Mom.

She nodded. "'That never would have happened if people would just lock their cars!'"

Chapter Eight

"That never would have happened if people would just lock their cars!" Dad said after we relayed the story to him that night over dinner.

The rest of us burst out laughing.

"I don't get it. Why is that funny?" Dad wanted to know, which only made us laugh harder. So predictable!

He took a sip of water. "So what do you think? Will they take the rose dress?"

"Your guess is as good as mine," Mom said. "We're just going to have to wait and see."

Dad cleared his throat. "You do know that even if Marcia does take the dress, it doesn't change the fact that we may still have to sell the store."

Mom and I exchanged glances.

"We understand," I said. "It's just the principle of the

thing. Fleur can't just take all the Homecoming business from us, you know?"

Dad nodded.

Still, I couldn't help hoping that saving at least part of the Homecoming business would make everyone realize things weren't quite so dire for the store.

I crossed my fingers for luck before I not-so-casually asked, "So how did *your* day go?"

Dad gave a small laugh. "Your great-aunt is quite a force to be reckoned with."

"Tell me about it," I said.

"She drove the realtor crazy. Nothing made her happy. One place was too big, the other too small. One didn't have enough parking. Another was too close to a clothing store that sold 'inappropriate attire for young ladies.'"

"She really said that?" asked Rose.

"That she did," said Dad. "She gave him quite a tongue-lashing for taking us there."

"Oh dear," said Mom. "The poor guy!"

In Spanish class on Monday, my phone suddenly vibrated in my pocket. I had a text message. My heart skipped a beat. I knew it had to be my mom, because all my friends were in class. And she would never text me during school unless it was something totally important — like she had heard from Marcia about the Homecoming dress! I briefly considered sneaking my phone open, but Señora Friedman was tough — using a cell phone in class meant instant detention. But I couldn't wait a whole forty minutes to read my text, either.

I raised my hand. Unfortunately, my timing was off. Señora Friedman thought I was volunteering to answer her next question.

"Señorita Bloom," said my teacher. "*¿Como se dice* 'she sleeps'?"

I thought for a minute. How *did* one say "she sleeps" in Spanish? Then it came to me. "*Duerme,*" I replied.

Señora Friedman smiled. "*Muy bien.*"

"May I, I mean . . ." I racked my brain. "*¿Puede . . . ir . . . al baño?*"

"*Puedo,*" my teacher corrected me. Then she nodded. "*Sí.*"

I practically skipped down the hallway in my excitement. In the restroom, I stood by the sink, the late afternoon sunlight struggling through the frosted-glass window. There, I flipped open my phone. Sure enough, the text was from my mom.

EVERYTHING IS COMING UP ROSES — THEY'RE TAKING THE DRESS! LOVE, MOM

"Wooo-hooo!" I cheered, which bounced around the tile-lined bathroom like an echo chamber. I cringed. Hopefully, no one had heard me!

Just then the toilet flushed and someone stepped out of the last stall. Someone with long, straight, brown hair, which she flipped over her shoulder. It was Sabrina, one of Ashley's henchwomen.

"I should have known it was you," she said. "Weirdo."

But I didn't care. Petal Pushers was back in business. I wore a huge smile as I walked back to class.

I wanted to run and tell Aster and Rose. I wanted to call Aunt Lily and tell her that we didn't need to sell the store after all. I imagined how gorgeous the dress would look at the parade. And then I had an evil thought: *Who's going to be looking at the bouquets when* that *dress is on the float?*

I grinned, feeling just a tiny bit guilty when I thought of Hamilton.

At lunch, I told my friends the good news.

"That's amazing!" said Amy.

"Good for you!" said Becky.

"Nice!" said Jessica.

Heather, as usual, had one thing on her mind — boys. "And now you can ask Hamilton out!" she concluded.

I held up a hand. "Give me a minute," I begged. "My head is still spinning!"

I unwrapped my turkey sandwich with cranberry mayo and ate it quickly. But I was still hungry, so Becky and I headed to the lunch line to get chocolate-chip cookies. On my way, I bumped into Rose.

"Great news!" I told her excitedly. "Mom texted me — they took the rose dress!"

"That's great," said Rose distractedly.

I grabbed her arm. "It *is* great. So why aren't you more excited?"

Rose shrugged.

"Hey, I didn't know you had third period lunch today," I told her. Sixth graders' lunch schedule changed every day. "You should have sat with us."

"Oh, it's okay," said Rose. "I'm fine." She waved toward a table in the back. "I had friends to sit with."

"Oh, good!" I said.

"How do you like being in middle school?" asked Becky. "Everything you dreamed it would be?" she added teasingly.

"Totes," Rose said. "Catch you guys later!"

Becky gave me a funny look as Rose walked off. I shrugged. *Totes?* Where had *that* come from?

"So has the realtor found any more places for you to see?" Mom asked Dad that night after dinner.

We were all lounging in the living room, waiting for our houseguests to arrive. Debbie and Nicholas had landed, picked up their rental car, and were on their way to our house. Mom was still knitting that scarf for Aster. Rose and Aster were playing Crazy Eights. I was finishing up my reading for history class tomorrow. And Dad and Poppy were huddled over his phone, as usual, harvesting beans and buying new farm equipment.

No reply.

"Honey, I said, did you talk to the realtor?" Mom's voice rose a bit.

Dad looked up. "Yes, I spoke to him. . . ."

Just then Poppy let out a piercing squeal and shoved the phone in Dad's face. "Look — it's a new kind of bean to plant — jelly beans!"

"Hey, look at that!" Dad said excitedly.

Mom threw a pillow at Dad. He and Poppy looked up at Mom, blinking slowly.

"*Jelly beans*, Mom!" Poppy explained.

Mom shook her head. "Forget it," she said. "We'll talk later, Ben. Go back to your silly game." She grinned ruefully and returned to her knitting.

Soon after, we heard a car pull in to the driveway.

"They're here!" Mom cheered, jumping off the couch so quickly she dropped Aster's scarf on the floor.

I glanced over at Dad, expecting a sympathetic look. Nicholas was here. But he and Poppy didn't look up from his phone.

Mom threw open the front door and gave Debbie a huge hug. Tall and big-boned, with thick chestnut hair, Debbie was the picture of good health. Mom said she ran ten miles a day.

"Deb-Deb!" Mom cried.

"Daisy Girl!"

My eyes widened in surprise. Goofy nicknames — how embarrassing!

"You look amazing!" Debbie gushed.

"No, *you* look amazing!" Mom insisted.

"Actually," said a voice from behind them with a slight Texas twang, "you both look pretty amazing!"

"Nicholas!" Mom cried. "How big and handsome you are!"

"No, *you're* big and handsome!" said Aster softly. I snickered.

I studied Nicholas as Mom gave him a hug. He was much taller than the last time I had seen him and his ears didn't look quite so huge anymore. He had straight dark hair and green eyes. A camera bag was slung around his neck.

"You remember Nicholas," Mom said to us. "And Nicholas, this is Ben, Rose, Aster, Del, and Poppy!"

Debbie gave us all big hugs and kisses and Nicholas shook everyone's hands rather formally. Then Mom brewed some tea and she and Debbie settled in on the couch and, as Gramps would say, took a walk down memory lane. They laughed and reminisced about their college days. Unfortunately, most of their stories didn't really make sense to anyone but them.

"Too much talking!" Poppy said crossly. "We're harvesting!" That was Dad's cue to scoop Poppy up over his shoulder and carry her upstairs to bed. Rose and Aster followed shortly after.

I glanced over at Nicholas, who sat on the couch, fiddling with his camera. "How was your trip?" I asked him politely.

"Actually," he said, "there was an extended period of turbulence on the plane, so it wasn't as enjoyable as I had anticipated."

"Oh . . . okay," I replied.

He nodded solemnly and returned to his camera.

"How is life in Texas?" Mom asked Debbie. "Tell me *everything*."

Yikes. This was *my* cue to head upstairs. "Can I show you to your room?" I asked Nicholas.

"Good idea, thanks," he said, yawning.

The steps creaked as we made our way upstairs.

"Old house," I explained.

"Actually, if you grate some Ivory Soap and put it between the creaky boards the noise will go away," he told me.

"Um, thanks," I replied.

I opened the door to his room, and Nicholas surveyed his surroundings. Full-sized bed. Plenty of pillows. A bed-side table and a lamp. What was he looking for? Finally, he nodded, satisfied.

"Good outlet-to-square-foot ratio," he said.

"Um — great!" I replied.

"Do I have my own bathroom?" he asked.

"You'll be sharing with your mom," I told him. "It's right across the hall."

"Acceptable," he said. He looked at his watch. "Okay, time for bed if I want to get my eight and a half hours," he told me, starting to shut the door. Then he poked his head out. "Del," he said, "I'm really looking forward to going to school with you tomorrow morning. We can discuss what I should wear over breakfast. Good night," he concluded, closing the door.

I stood there, blinking. Looking forward to going *where* with me tomorrow? This had to be a joke!

Chapter Nine

Unfortunately, it was not a joke at all.

When I got to the breakfast table the next morning, there sat Nicholas, wrapped up in a plaid bathrobe, eating a bowl of cereal.

"Today's the day!" he said. "I can't wait."

I didn't know what to say. I walked over to the refrigerator and pulled out a carton of orange juice.

"You want any?" I asked our houseguest.

"Actually," he said, "I prefer a glass of tomato juice first thing in the morning. You don't happen to have any, do you?"

I shook my head. "Sorry." I picked up the box of cereal to discover it felt awfully light. I looked inside. Empty. Hmmm.

Mom walked into the room, and I gave her the evil

eye. "Nicholas informed me that he's coming to school with me today," I told her, my voice rising.

"Oh, that's right!" Mom said cheerily. "Did I forget to tell you? I've arranged the whole thing with your school." My mouth fell open, but Mom kept going. "Nicholas will be spending the morning with you, attending all your classes."

"I don't get it," I said.

She turned to Nicholas. "And then I'll pick you up right before lunch and you can help me out in the shop in the afternoon," she finished.

Wait — he was helping out at *Petal Pushers*?

"Sounds great," he said.

I turned to Nicholas. "But school is so boring! Wouldn't you rather spend the day with your mom sightseeing?" I suggested. "Don't forget — Tupperware!"

"My mom had to go to Boston this morning for business," he explained. "And actually, I've really been looking forward to seeing what middle school is like in New Hampshire! Your principal said I could bring my camera and take lots of pictures. I'm planning on doing a presentation when I get back to my school."

I shook my head. Was this really happening?

He frowned. "So, should I wear my blue pullover or my red cardigan?" he asked me. "I'd like to blend in, you know. As a photojournalist."

"Um . . . pullover," I said.

"I assume jeans are okay?" He took one last spoonful of cereal and headed upstairs.

As soon as he was gone, I glowered at my mom.

"What?" she said over her mug of coffee. "Oh, come on, it's not *that* big a deal, is it?"

"Actually," I said. "It is."

That made her laugh. "All right," she said with a sigh. "I owe you one."

"He ate the last bowl of Oatie-os," I said. "You owe me *two*."

I was waiting at the bottom of the stairs, as usual. Nicholas came down first in the red cardigan, a perfectly pressed white oxford shirt, and a blue-and-red-striped tie. He wore jeans and penny loafers. Worst of all, his big, geeky camera was slung around his neck. He was going to blend in at school about as easily as someone wearing a clown costume.

Rose came down next. "Are you really planning on going to school dressed like that?" she asked.

"Rose!" said Aster, who had quietly slipped downstairs after her. "That's mean."

At first, I thought she was talking to Nicholas. But she was eyeing me directly. I glanced down at the cute red kilt and black turtleneck I was wearing. What was she talking about?

"Um . . . yeah," I said to Rose. Why was she suddenly being so critical of my clothes? Weird.

But I quickly forgot about it as the four of us set off for school. Nicholas chatted away about the photos he would take for his photo essay comparing and contrasting the middle school experience in Austin versus Elwood Falls, pausing only to wonder aloud if we were taking the most direct route to school. Should we have made a left on Hawthorne instead of Hickory? It looked that way when he had looked it up on MapQuest the night before. I sighed as he rambled on.

Once we arrived, Aster gave me a sympathetic look as she headed to her locker. Rose waved at me with a smirk. "Good luck!" she said.

"Are you sure that's the most efficient way to organize your locker?" Nicholas asked me as I jerked open the lock. "Alphabetically? Have you considered chronologically?" He took off his lens cap and began snapping away.

When I didn't answer, he added, "You know what I mean, right? The order that your classes are in?"

"I am well aware of what *chronologically* means," I said between clenched teeth.

Nicholas snapped a picture of me, lowered his camera, and examined the shot. "Not the best look for you," he said. "I guess I'll delete that one. You really should smile more."

And, once we arrived in the cafeteria: "Are you sure you want hot chocolate? That's a lot of sugar first thing in the morning. I'm sure they must have green tea. Lots of antioxidants." He focused his camera on the display of breakfast cereals. *Snap, snap, snap.*

I could feel my jaw clenching. This was going to be one long morning. Then I spotted a familiar face from across the room. Hamilton. He was laughing with a friend. My cheeks got hot and I turned away quickly.

After Nicholas had taken an action shot of the lunch

lady serving up some oatmeal, we headed over to see my friends.

"This is Nicholas," I said. "He lives in Austin and he's staying with us for a couple of days. His mom went to McIlhenny University with my mom." I smiled. "Perhaps you're all not aware that today is Take-a-Texan-to-School Day."

"Nope," laughed Heather. "I guess you'll have to share him, Del!"

"Hi, Nicholas," said Becky, looking like she was trying hard not to laugh. I had texted her, filling her in on our new visitor before bed last night.

"Welcome to Sarah Josepha Hale Middle School," said Amy.

Jessica bit her lip. "I had no idea it was Take-a-Texan-to-School Day," she said.

"Actually," said Nicholas. "I had no idea Del had such lovely friends!"

I rolled my eyes. Nicholas was about as annoying as a person could possibly be.

"Awwwww," said my friends. Apparently, they did not agree with me.

"Do you mind if I take some photographs of you guys?" he asked. "It's for a school project."

"No problem!" said Heather, fluffing her hair and smiling prettily. "Cheese!"

Things got worse in history class. Nicholas raised his hand more than I did.

He answered questions I didn't know the answers to. About the decline of the mills in New Hampshire, no less. And I had done the reading the night before. *And* taken notes.

I looked at him in disbelief. "How do you know this stuff?" I whispered.

"Actually, I checked out the New Hampshire middle-school curriculum online and did some research," he whispered back.

"Very informative," said my teacher, Mr. Decker. I was stunned. Even my most well-researched homework answers hadn't gotten more than a "fine" from my tough teacher. This was worse than I had expected.

In Spanish class, Nicholas conversed with Señora Friedman in perfect Spanish and she commended him on his Castilian accent. By the time that class was over, I was officially done with my "shadow." I practically ran out the door, I was in such a rush to get rid of my special visitor. I turned around impatiently to see why he was dawdling to discover that he was chatting away with someone. I took a closer look. Yikes — it was Sabrina, one of Ashley's best friends. *Oh no,* I thought. *He's embarrassing me in front of one of her handmaidens! Social suicide.*

He held up his camera, and Sabrina grinned and struck a pose.

I ducked back, grabbed his hand, and pulled him away from Sabrina and down the hall. "My mom is waiting!" I told him. "Can't be late!"

He shut off his camera and rubbed his hands together. "Well, that was great!" he said. "I think I made a good impression. Probably scored you some brownie points with your teachers, too." I ground my teeth in annoyance. "And all the kids seem so nice! Sabrina is really pretty, don't you think?"

"Whatever," I said.

"Hey, Delphinium!" a voice shouted. "Who's your Siamese twin?"

I would recognize that obnoxious voice anywhere. It was Bob, the school bully and my second-worst enemy (after Ashley, of course).

"Ignore him," I told Nicholas.

But Nicholas could not resist the lure of correcting someone's mistake. He stopped short and turned to face Bob. "Actually," Nicholas told him, "the preferred term is *conjoined twin*."

Bob stared at him like he was insane.

"The term 'Siamese twin' originated, of course, from Chang and Eng Bunker," Nicholas explained.

Still no response from Bob, who was beginning to look alarmed.

"The conjoined twins from Thailand?" Nicholas asked incredulously. "They shared a liver, you know!"

Bob blinked.

Nicholas shook his head in exasperation. "Of course, you know that Thailand was formerly known as *Siam*?" he explained as if Bob was a dimwitted child. As annoying as Nicholas was, I couldn't help enjoying the confused look on Bob's face.

I touched Nicholas's arm, bringing him back to reality.

"My mom is waiting," I told him. "Say good-bye to your new friend Bob."

As we walked down the hall, Nicholas shook his head. "Philistine!" he said. I had no idea what that meant, but if it was about Bob, I assumed it wasn't good.

"Philistine!" I agreed.

I marched Nicholas out the front door, and down the stone steps of the school. Luckily, Mom's car was there waiting. "Have fun at the store today," I told him before I slammed the car door shut. I waved as Mom drove off.

Then I breathed a sigh of relief. I had enjoyed the scene with Bob, but there were only so many *actuallys* a girl could take in one day.

I rushed down the hallway toward the cafeteria. It was chicken-finger-and-waffle-fries day and I was already ten minutes late thanks to my camera-happy buddy. Just then, my phone began to vibrate. I paused for a minute, reached into my pocket, and flipped it open.

I had a text. From Nicholas!

WANNA MEET UP AFTER SCHOOL? he'd written.

Was he for real? We had literally been apart for two minutes!

2 BUSY. I wrote back. C U L8TR.

"How did it go?" Becky asked as I sat down with my lunch, feeling victorious because I had nabbed the very last serving of chicken fingers. I dunked a crispy finger into the barbecue sauce. Pure crunchy deliciousness.

I shook my head. "He thinks he knows everything. He wouldn't stop taking pictures. How could my mom do that to me?"

"Well, I just heard he called Bob the Philly Fanatic," said Jessica. "And Bob was mad."

"Something like that," I said with a grin.

"So his visit wasn't a total disaster," said Heather.

"I guess not," I admitted. But it didn't change the fact that I was counting down the days until our visitors returned to Texas.

That afternoon, Aster and I walked home from school together. Rose had rehearsal and Dad would be picking her up after his office hours.

I vented about Nicholas, and Aster was quiet, as usual. Then she asked, "Do you really think we're going to have to sell the store?"

I felt the familiar pang as soon as I thought about our family business becoming a trendy coffee shop. "I don't know, Aster. I sure hope not."

"There's something else that's bothering me," she said. "Del, I'm worried about Rose."

I nodded. "She has been acting weird lately. Kind of rude."

Aster shoved her hands into her pockets. "And sad," she said. "I miss the old Rose."

"I know," I told her. "But I wouldn't worry. She's going through a rough patch. Not getting the role she wanted in the play. And I think she might be a little jealous of your new friends. She's used to being the popular one. It will work itself out."

"You really think so?" Aster said. "It's just weird — she was part of this big group of friends in our old school, but they don't seem to hang out together anymore. I think maybe she's . . . lonely."

I looked at her worried, pale face, framed by her dark hair. I smiled. "She's Rose. Everything will be fine. She'll make new friends. We just have to give her time."

"I hope you're right," said Aster.

When we got home, Aster headed upstairs and I went into the kitchen, where I found Mom, Nicholas, Poppy, and Debbie all bunched around a laptop.

"We're looking at Nicholas's photos," said Mom. "Come see. They're incredible!"

"I uploaded the pictures from today at your school," Nicholas told me.

He put on a little slide show for us. There I was, shelving my books in my locker. Alphabetically. There was the lunch lady, a big grin on her face as she handed over the oatmeal. The back of a kid looking out a window at the swirling fall leaves. A close-up of my science teacher, all bushy eyebrows and bow tie, his finger in the air making an important point. Two girls whispering together, a look of surprise on the second girl's face.

They were good. Very good.

"You have quite an eye, Nicholas," said Mom.

And there was a picture of me in the cafeteria that morning. I hadn't realized it had been taken. I had a funny, faraway look in my eyes.

"What was I . . ." I started to ask.

"Oh, that's when you were staring at that guy —"

"Who was eating that really big . . . bagel!" I finished lamely, my cheeks burning. I knew exactly which guy I was staring at. Hamilton.

I wanted to change the subject. Immediately. "So, let's see some of your other work," I said.

"Show the ones from the football game we went to last weekend," Debbie suggested.

"Good idea," said Nicholas. He opened up another folder and started another slide show.

There was a close-up of a cheerleader in mid-yell. A dazed-looking football player, his helmet in his hands. A shouting girl, her face painted half red and half white, wearing the hugest . . .

I jabbed my finger at the screen. "Wait! What *is* that?" I asked.

Nicholas stopped the slide show and returned to the photo in question.

"Holy guacamole!" said Poppy. We all stared in disbelief. The girl was wearing the largest corsage I had ever seen in my life. It was covered with ribbons and trinkets. It was way too big to pin on, so it hung around her neck like an enormous necklace. And it was made with fake flowers.

"That's a mum corsage," explained Nicholas.

"But it's so . . . huge," Mom said.

Debbie laughed. "You know what they say — everything is bigger in Texas!"

I studied the ginormous corsage, an idea beginning to form.

"Hey!" said Nicholas. "Why doesn't Petal Pushers make mum corsages to sell at the big game?" he asked.

"No, wait," I protested. "That's what I was thinking!"

"What a great idea, Nicholas!" said Rose, smirking at me.

Mom grimaced. "I don't know. I'm not sure if such huge corsages are going to go over so well here in preppy New England."

"I think you should give it a try," Nicholas insisted.

I smiled. I had an idea. A really good idea. "I'll be back in a minute!" I said.

I rushed into the dining room, where Mom's Homecoming bouquet, now slightly wilted, still sat in a vase. I grabbed two of the less bedraggled-looking roses — an orange and a yellow — and trimmed the stems. I plucked out the two prettiest preserved leaves I could find. Then I pulled the hair elastic out from around my ponytail, and wrapped it tightly around the stems.

I ran back into the kitchen where everyone was still debating over whether the citizens of Elwood Falls were ready for massive fake corsages.

I held the corsage up to my chest. "Ta-da!" I said. "It's the official 'Coming Up Roses' Homecoming corsage! Just imagine that this orange rose is red and you've got the school colors! We can make up a bunch and sell them right before the game!"

Mom's mouth fell open. "Del! It's perfect!" Her eyes were shining. "And you even found a way to use the leaves!"

Nicholas nodded. "Good thing I'm here, huh?"

I was too excited to get annoyed with him. "Yeah," I said. "Good thing."

Chapter Ten

Things really were looking up for the Blooms. When it looked like we were being left out of Homecoming, we had managed to create not one, but two innovative new ways to be involved. I should have been happy.

But I couldn't help worrying. What if the corsages were a big flop? What if something went wrong with the rose dress? What if Aunt Lily convinced everyone we needed to sell the store?

It was Wednesday, three days before the big day. *At least,* I thought to myself on my way to school that morning, *you don't have to bring Mr. Know-It-All to school with you today!* Thank goodness for small favors.

At lunchtime, I headed over to the drink machine to treat myself to an iced tea. I ran into my friend Maria

Gonzalez and chatted with her about her latest art project, a menagerie of animals she'd made entirely out of office supplies. Maria was so creative that I sometimes wished she worked at Petal Pushers — she'd be a natural!

After three tries to get the machine to take my dollar, I pressed the ICED TEA button. And out came a grape soda. Not my favorite by a long shot. I was standing there, deciding whether I had time to try to return the soda and get my money back, when a flash of perfectly straightened blonde hair caught my eye.

It was Ashley, talking animatedly with someone at a nearby table. But then I took another look. Ashley wasn't talking with either of her two interchangeable brunette best friends. This girl was younger and blonder.

My mouth fell open.

Ashley was having a conversation with my sister Rose!

It took a moment for it to sink in. Then it all started to make perfect sense. *Ashley* was the reason my sister was insulting my clothes and using words like "totes."

But why had Ashley befriended my younger sister? I took a swig of the grape soda, grimaced, and started to march over to confront them. But then the bell rang for class. I was blocked by the mass of students all standing up at the same exact time and swarming around the garbage cans. I felt like a salmon swimming its way upstream as I tried to fight through the crowd. By the time I ended up at the table my sister and my enemy had been sitting at, they were gone.

The only thing left was a napkin with a perfect, glittery pink lip-gloss kiss mark on it.

At the end of the day, I made my way to Ashley's locker. Her handmaidens stood on either side of her as she looked in her locker mirror and smoothed her already perfect hair. She turned around and looked me up and down. "Hello, Delphinium," she said snidely. "Need some fashion advice?"

"All I want to know is why you are hanging out with my little sister," I told her, getting right to the point.

"What's it to you?" Ashley asked.

"Yeah, like, what's it to you?" said Sabrina.

"The only reason I can see that you would want to

hang out with a sixth grader is to annoy me," I said. "So I'm going to ask you nicely. Why are you spending time with Rose?"

Ashley smirked. "Why don't you ask her yourself?" she said, pointing behind me.

My heart sank. This was not going the way I had planned it. I turned around, wincing, and there stood Rose at her locker, which, I just realized, was directly across the hall from Ashley's. She did not look happy at all.

"Aren't you supposed to be at rehearsal?" I asked her.

Ashley snorted. "Shows how much you know about your own sister," she said. "She quit ages ago!"

I couldn't believe what I had just heard. "Rose, is that true?"

Rose ignored my question, her cheeks turning bright pink. "Is it too difficult to think that Ashley is hanging out with me because she likes me, Del?" she asked.

Actually, it was. Unfortunately, when the word *actually* popped into my mind, I thought of Nicholas and how he seemed to be trying to set a world record for the number of times he could say that word, and it made me smile.

Rose's mouth fell open. "This isn't funny, Del!" she said angrily. "You think everything is about you. And it isn't!"

She stormed down the hall. Ashley grinned at me. "I'm going to go see how my dear friend Rose is doing," she said, slamming her locker shut and sauntering off.

I stood there, shaking. It all made sense now. Rose had been having a rough time in middle school. Especially since Aster was, shockingly enough, fitting in so well. Even the Drama Club, where Rose had always been a star, had been a disappointment to her. Ashley, I reasoned, must have figured out who Rose was, seen her looking upset, and decided she'd "befriend" her. It was just my bad luck that their lockers were so close.

I had to convince Rose that Ashley was no friend of hers. And that she couldn't just give up on Drama Club after one disappointment — acting was her biggest love! Plus, I knew that if she followed her passion, she'd find *real* friends.

But it was going to be hard. Because right now I didn't think my sister was talking to me.

Wouldn't you know it, as I was standing there, trying

to collect my thoughts, I got another text message from Nicholas.

HEY — R U GOING TO HOMECOMING?

Was he for real? Enough was enough. Angrily, I typed back: WHAT DO YOU THINK, EINSTEIN?

Could this day get any more annoying?

Chapter Eleven

I woke up Friday morning and lay in bed for approximately one split second before my brain started to swirl with activity. I had a lot on my plate today:

1) Get Rose to talk to me (last night over dinner had been a complete failure) and explain to her that Ashley was a big fake. Oh, and get her to rejoin Drama Club.
2) Pass my Spanish test.
3) Rush to the store right after school to start assembling hundreds of Homecoming corsages. And hope, hope, hope that we would be able to sell them.
4) Try not to fixate too much on the big family meeting on Sunday about the future of Petal Pushers.

5) And finally — try to figure out why was Hamilton Baldwin was not talking to me.

Things had been really weird yesterday at school. He passed me in the hall and didn't seem to see me. He didn't pass my locker once all day. Had he decided to take an alternate route to avoid me? And during assembly, I waved to him from across the auditorium and he had pretended he hadn't seen me! So *I'd* pretended I was fixing my hair, my face burning with embarrassment.

"He must have heard that we were trying to take back some of the Homecoming business from his mom's store," I had said to my friends that day at lunch. "And now he's mad."

Becky had shaken her head. "That makes no sense," she'd said. "He has no interest in what goes on in either flower shop. He told you that himself."

I sighed. "But then what could it be?"

"Maybe he's just in a bad mood," said Jessica with a shrug.

Well, whatever was going on was certainly starting to put *me* in one.

As Becky would, I tried to look on the bright side. I'd be so busy on Saturday that it was probably better that Hamilton wouldn't be going to the game with me.

Somehow, this thought did not make me feel any better.

I made myself get up and get dressed. Downstairs, my family — and Nicholas and his mom — were all gathered around the breakfast table.

"Please pass the maple syrup, Nicholas," Rose said pointedly as I took my seat.

"Really, Rose?" I said. The maple syrup was sitting right next to my plate.

"Really," she said. I shook my head and handed Nicholas the syrup, who then handed it to Rose. "Thank you, Nicholas," she said.

Aster looked at me, concerned.

On the walk to school, for the first time ever, Rose walked so quickly she was soon a block ahead of us.

"What's going on?" Aster asked. "Why is Rose so mad at you?"

"I . . . um . . . found out that she has been hanging

out with Ashley Edwards. And I think she dropped out of Drama Club entirely."

Aster's eyes widened. "Why?"

I shrugged. "To hang out with her new BFF?"

"But why would Ashley want to hang out with Rose?" Aster wondered.

"I think it's to get back at me," I said. "But Rose heard me telling Ashley that, and now she's furious with me."

Aster shook her head. "This is bad," she said. "What can we do about it?" Her shoulders sagged. "I've been a terrible sister."

I shook my head. "I need to figure out a way to convince Rose that she doesn't want to hang out with Ashley. It has to be *her* decision, though."

Aster frowned. "I told you something was wrong," she said.

I sighed. "I know, Aster. I should have listened. I guess I was too distracted by everything else that's been going on."

When we got to school, we went our separate ways. "Good luck," said Aster. "Let me know what I can do."

"I will," I promised. But I had absolutely no idea what *I* was going to do, let alone how anyone else could help.

❁ ❁ ❁

But in the middle of English class I had a sudden, brilliant idea.

Mrs. Ferrerio had been going around the room, calling on students to take turns reading from the Shakespeare play we were studying, *Romeo and Juliet.* I sighed. This was going to be one painful class.

And at first, I was right. Most kids mumbled their lines, or read them like they were grocery lists instead of dialogue. I was alternating between being hugely bored and totally nervous that I would be called on next when Lisa Davis and Maryann Williams began to read a scene between Juliet and her Nurse. I began to listen. Lisa was funny and feisty as the Nurse. I even laughed out loud.

"Excellent!" Mrs. Ferrerio said, a smile finally spreading across her face.

Then the bell rang, and I was spared having to follow up Lisa's amazing delivery. I picked up my books and fought through the crowd to catch up with her in the hallway. This couldn't be more perfect — Lisa had the lead in the school play. Plus, she had been in elementary school with me and Ashley. I knew how to win Rose back from the dark side. I just hoped Lisa would go along with it.

Finally, the day was over. Lisa was going to meet me at my locker and we would head over to pay Ashley a visit. Hopefully, Rose would show up soon after.

When we arrived, Rose, Sabrina, Rachel, and Ashley were all whispering together at Ashley's locker. "Hello, Ashley," I said. She turned, looking surprised to see me standing there with Lisa.

"Well, hello, Delphinium, Linda," she said.

"Lisa," Lisa corrected her.

"Whatev," Ashley said. "What do you geeks, I mean, girls, want?" Sabrina and Rachel laughed. Rose shifted, looking uncomfortable.

"Hey, Rose," said Lisa. "We missed you at rehearsal yesterday."

"Rose has more important things to do," said Ashley. "Right, Rose?"

"Um . . . yeah," said Rose.

"She's not into acting anymore," Ashley explained for her.

"It's funny," I said directly to Rose. "Lisa and I remember when *Ashley* used to be really into acting."

"That's right," said Lisa. "She even got the lead in the third-grade play."

"You did?" Rose asked Ashley. "I thought you said acting was for losers."

Ashley looked down at her admittedly fabulous pair of clog boots. "That was a long time ago," she said.

"Ashley couldn't remember any of her lines," I went on, "and Lisa had to whisper them to her. Then she walked off the stage in the middle of the first act and Lisa had to play two parts!"

"I quit the play because it was lame!" Ashley insisted.

"So, Rose," I said. "It's not that Ashley thinks Drama Club is for losers, it's that she hates drama. Because she wasn't very good at it."

Ashley snapped open her locker. "That's not true," she said with a sneer. "I really do think it's totes for losers."

Ugh. Of all of Ashley's abbreviations, that one had to be the worst! I cleared my throat, about to lecture my sister. "I know it's been hard not having the lead role. But next year, I'm sure you'll get a bigger part. And before you know it . . ."

"Zip it, Del," said Rose. She smiled at me. "You've convinced me. Thank you." My mouth fell open as Rose turned to Lisa and the two began chatting as they walked down the hallway.

Ashley stared after my sister, her hands on her hips, her mouth set into a thin line. Then she shrugged and spun open her lock. "Whatev," she said. She turned to me. "You still here? Um, do you mind moving away from my locker? I don't want people to think we're hanging out or anything."

"With pleasure, Paris Hilton," I said, naming the worst actress I could think of.

Ashley looked at me blankly. It didn't matter that she had no idea what I had meant. It felt good to me. So I took off after Rose and Lisa. I tapped Rose on the shoulder and she and Lisa turned around.

Lisa beamed at me. "Rose is coming back to Drama Club!" she said.

"That's great," I told them both. I grinned at Rose. "Was I really that persuasive?" I couldn't help asking.

Rose bit her lip. "Oh, maybe a little," she said. "Well, what really happened was that Aster and her goth friends walked by yesterday and Ashley started making fun of them. I told her to lay off and she wouldn't. That is so totally uncool." She took a deep breath. "Plus, I missed going to rehearsal, even though I wasn't the star. And I met a fun girl in my math class. We're going to the mall together on Sunday."

"Oh good," I said, feeling slightly deflated. I guess I wasn't quite as helpful as I had imagined. Still, things were back to normal, and that was all that mattered, anyway.

Rose gave me a quick hug. "I do appreciate your looking out for me, Del," she said.

"Of course," I said. I watched as she and Lisa headed to rehearsal. That was one less person to help with the corsage making this afternoon. But it was totally worth it.

I packed up my books and went to collect Aster at her locker.

"Rose won't be joining us today," I told her. "She's at rehearsal!"

"Oh, Del, that's great!" Aster said. "I knew you could do it!"

"Actually, I think Rose figured it out for herself," I told her.

"Hello, everyone!" I called out as I pushed open the flower shop door. The bell rang merrily.

"Hello, Delphinium, Aster," said Aunt Lily. My stomach sank. She, Mom, Debbie, and Nicholas were sitting at the worktable. They were surrounded by leaves, yellow and red roses, floral wire, tape, and corsage pins. My great-aunt was dressed in a tweedy suit as usual, but her hat and jacket were off and the sleeves of her pale blue silk blouse were rolled up. There was a pile of expertly made corsages next to her.

"Hey, Aunt Lily," I said. "Did you make those corsages?"

She nodded, smiling. "It comes right back to you!" she said, indicating the pile. "Like riding a bike!"

I caught Mom's eye and she gave me a tiny shrug back as if to say, *Your guess is as good as mine!*

"Don't just stand there, you guys," said Nicholas. "Pull up a chair!" I slipped off my jacket, and Aster and I joined in.

We laughed and joked, put roses in our hair, and

listened as Nicholas told us about the history of the corsage. A lump formed in my throat as I looked from Mom to Aster. This could be one of the last times we worked together in the old store.

When I thought we were done, Mom hauled out two more buckets of roses — one red, one yellow.

"What's going on?" I asked.

Mom shrugged. "Nicholas was here when I was ordering the roses and he convinced me to order extra. He's really sure we're going to sell each and every one."

I gave him a questioning look, but he just smiled at me.

"You can thank me later, Del," he said.

Finally, my cramped fingers wrapped the very last floral wire around my very last corsage. We were done. Yawning, I collected the empty pizza boxes and soda cans left over from our hasty supper.

At home, as I climbed into bed, I had one last thought before I fell into a deep sleep: *Can everything go smoothly, just for once?*

Chapter Twelve

The next morning, we drove to Petal Pushers to assemble the rose dress. On the way there, I got a small thrill of excitement. It was Homecoming Day! The town was already bustling with activity, and a huge sign hung over Fairfield Street read WELCOME TO HOMECOMING WEEKEND! In all the drama, I had lost sight of the fun that was in store.

I wasn't going with Hamilton, but other than that, everything would be okay. As long as we got the dress done in time, and people bought corsages, what could go wrong?

Approximately four hundred roses later, Mom was finished. She had hired a seamstress to make a simple, floor-length strapless dress out of a light, yet sturdy fabric. And then Mom had completely covered the dress with roses.

I helped her place the rose-covered garment on the dress form. We stepped across the room and took our first real look at our creation.

Dad let out a low whistle. "I think you've outdone yourselves," he said.

"Oh, Mom," I breathed. "It's incredible."

"It is," she said in a hushed voice.

It was the most beautiful dress I had ever seen, covered in velvety soft, red buds. It looked like the richest, softest fabric that money could buy. And the smell was heavenly. I just wanted to bury my face in it. I felt this warm glow of pride spreading out in my chest. It had been an amazing idea, if I did say so myself.

Nicholas, of course, took several shots of it, from all different angles. After we packed up the corsages, each one nestled into a cardboard display, Mom hung the dress on a padded hanger. We'd be transporting it on a dress rack in the back of the van. Nicholas had volunteered to sit in the back and make sure it didn't get crushed. To be safe, Mom packed a whole bunch of replacement red roses.

Mom, Nicholas, Rose, Aster, and I piled into the minivan. Dad drove Debbie and Poppy in his car. We'd all rendezvous in the parking lot at McIlhenny University.

Rose and Aster were in the middle seats, whispering excitedly to each other. For once, their extreme closeness didn't make me feel the slightest bit wistful. I was just happy things were back to normal with them.

I peered out the window as we approached the campus. Crowds were milling about, wearing their McIlhenny sweatshirts. A bunch of kids were wearing moose antlers on their heads. Others had their faces painted half red and half yellow.

"Wow, it's so crowded already," I said nervously as we pulled up. We had a special pass to park in the faculty lot, and the guard waved us in.

"Let's set everyone up with the corsages first," said Mom. "Then we can deliver the dress to Marcia."

We parked and began unloading the corsages. Dad pulled up shortly after and parked his car nearby. Debbie, Nicholas, Rose, and Aster each got a display.

"They're ten dollars each," I told them. "Three for twenty-five."

Dad volunteered to keep an eye on things while

Mom and I helped everyone find the best locations. Nicholas claimed the front gate. "McIlhenny Moose Corsages!" he immediately began to cry. "Get 'em while they're hot!"

Aster promised to watch Poppy at their spot by the south entrance. Debbie picked the area by the ticket booth. Rose picked the restrooms. "Everybody's got to go at some point," she said. I had to give her that.

People began lining up for the corsages almost immediately. Mrs. McGillicuddy, whose anniversary party we had done over the summer, grabbed my arm. "What a great idea, Del!" she cried. "I adore the fall leaves. How in the world did you preserve them so beautifully?"

"Paraffin," I told her. "Mom's idea."

I looked over at Debbie. She had a long line in front of her, too. "We'd better drop off that dress and start bringing these guys more corsages!" I exclaimed.

"Nicholas was right!" Mom said.

"I guess he was," I admitted.

We headed back to the parking lot. There was Dad, leaning against his car, concentrating on his iPhone. The van was nowhere to be seen.

Mom walked up to him. "Ben, this isn't the time for jokes," she said. "Where's the van?"

Dad looked up. "Huh? What are you talking about?"

"Have you been playing that Gnome game the whole time?" I asked.

Dad looked sheepish. "Yes," he said. "It was time to harvest my navy beans. You know I hate it when they wither."

I took a deep breath. "Well, if you haven't noticed . . . the van isn't here!"

"Someone must have stolen it from right under your nose!" Mom cried.

Dad looked around wildly. Then he smiled and pointed. "No, there it is!" he said. "You just forgot where you parked it!"

I looked at Mom. Was that possible? I was fairly certain we had parked it next to the red sports car. But there sat the white van, a couple of rows away.

Mom shook her head. "That's weird. I could have sworn it was parked closer to Dad's car . . . I guess we're just worked up. I, for one, won't be able to relax until the dress is delivered to Marcia."

"And the corsages are all sold," I added.

"That, too," said Mom.

Mom gave Dad a dirty look and he wisely pocketed his phone. We walked up to the van. It looked dirtier than I remembered and someone had traced *WASH ME* into the dust on the back window. I hadn't noticed that when we loaded up that morning.

Dad threw open the back door.

And it was completely empty.

"Someone stole our rose dress!" said Mom. "And the rest of our corsages!"

The campus police officer looked very confused as he took down our report. "So you say that someone moved your van and then stole a dress with roses on it?"

"No, the dress is *made* of roses," I explained.

"Um, come again?" the officer said politely.

Nicholas came jogging up to us. "Everyone wants corsages! I need more," he said. Then he noticed the looks on our faces, and the police officer. "What's going on?" he asked.

My heart was beating superfast and my hands were shaking. "Someone stole the rose dress!" I cried.

Mom wrung her hands. "I'm supposed to get the dress to Marcia in fifteen minutes," she said. "What am I going to tell her?"

"Who would do something like that?" Nicholas asked. Then his eyes narrowed. "I'll bet it was those people from Fleur! They must have heard about your amazing dress and now they're trying to sabotage you!"

"That's crazy!" I said. But then I wondered, *Or is it?*

"You don't really think that's what happened, do you?" Dad asked Mom.

"I don't know what I think right now," Mom said, sniffling. She searched her pockets and came up empty. "And I forgot my bandanna!"

I felt sick. Was the competition between our stores so intense that things had come to this? My heart sank as I thought the unthinkable — could Hamilton have something to do with this? It was too horrible to consider.

"Must be some students who took the van on a joyride," Dad said.

The campus police officer nodded. "We do have a lot of high jinks on campus this time of year," he agreed. "Last night someone put a huge pair of moose antlers on the statue of Vern McIlhenny."

"Or maybe," I mused, "it was someone from the other team."

"You think one of the Benton Beavers fans stole our van?" Mom asked.

"They could be trying to sabotage the Homecoming parade," Dad said.

Mom sniffed again. I remembered that I had left a pack of tissues in the car. I opened the passenger-side door and pulled open the glove compartment. An avalanche of Three Musketeers bars spilled out.

"Huh?" I said. I will never understand the appeal of a Three Musketeers. It's a Milky Way without the caramel. (And, obviously, a Milky Way is a Snickers without the peanuts.) I grabbed one and ran to my mom and dad, who were still trying to explain what had happened to the officer.

"So let me get this straight for once and for all. You're saying that the owner of the stolen dress is named Rose?" the officer asked.

"Look!" I cried, holding out a candy bar.

Mom gave me a what-in-the-world-are-you-thinking look. "Del, this is no time to have a snack," she said.

"No," I said. "This isn't our van. This van belongs to someone who loves the taste of fluffy nougat."

Dad looked at the license plate and his jaw dropped. "Oh wow," he said. "You're right. This isn't our van."

The officer smiled. "Now we're getting somewhere," he said. "Your van was stolen by someone wearing a dress."

"Actually," said Nicholas, "I don't think your van was stolen at all. And I think we can get it back pretty easily."

As Nicholas explained, he was a big fan of a radio show called *Car Talk*. And last week he had learned that keys of cars of the same make and model can start each other. "So all we have to do is find out who drives the same car as you," Nicholas concluded.

Dad was nodding. "I know who took it," he said. "The assistant dean." He laughed. "He must have just gotten into the van and driven off, not realizing it wasn't his. He and his wife just had a baby. So he's been a little distracted lately."

"I hope he's a careful driver!" Mom worried. "He doesn't know he has the world's most fragile dress bouncing around in the back!"

After a few tense moments, we got the assistant dean's cell number. He didn't pick up and Dad left him the world's strangest message. "Um, excuse me, Dean Washington, I think you accidentally stole my minivan with a dress made out of roses in the back. . . ."

By then, the whole family had returned to the parking lot looking for more corsages. So there was quite a crowd by the time Dean Washington pulled into the parking lot, honking his horn.

He looked totally embarrassed. "Ben!" he said as he got out of the car. "How in the world did this happen? I can't even begin to apologize!"

Mom rushed over and threw open the back door of the van. "The dress is fine!" she called.

"Yay!" everyone cheered.

"You know we just had a baby girl," the assistant dean

explained. “I’m a little sleep deprived, as you can imagine.” Everyone nodded sympathetically. “I got here early to get ready for the parade when I got an emergency call from my wife that we were out of diapers. I hopped into the first white van I saw. I was so distracted I didn’t even notice it wasn’t my van until you called.”

He shook his head ruefully. “Who ever heard of your keys being able to start someone else’s car?”

“Actually,” I said, “he did.” I pointed to Nicholas, who smiled.

Everyone grabbed new corsages to sell. Mom and I gingerly picked up the dress and rushed it over to the auditorium, where the Homecoming Queen and her court would be getting dressed.

Marcia was standing by the door. “You made it!” she said. “I was getting worried! Did something happen?”

Mom and I looked at each other and laughed. “If we told you, you’d never believe it,” I said.

Marcia brought the dress over to the Homecoming Queen, who happened to be Emily, the girl we had first met in Marcia’s office. We waited until Emily put it on to make sure it fit. Mom had extra roses and her sewing kit at the ready just in case.

Then Emily came out wearing the dress. It was the first time we had seen the completed dress on an actual person. It looked so luxurious, so beautiful, so velvety soft, and it smelled so fragrant, it took everyone's breath away.

"Wow," I said. There was nothing else to say.

Emily looked down at the flowing red, textured skirt. She laughed delightedly. "It's a little heavy," she said. "But who cares? I feel like a . . . a . . ."

"Homecoming Queen?" I suggested.

She laughed. "The coolest Homecoming Queen ever," she said.

As we walked back to the van, I suddenly realized how exhausted I was.

"Me too!" said Mom when I told her. "What a stressful morning!"

"Shall we sell some corsages?" I suggested.

"Good idea," replied Mom.

But when we got to the van, the back was empty.

My heart stopped. "Do you think . . ."

"We sold every one," said Nicholas from behind us. "They were a huge hit! We could have used a hundred more!"

"Looks like we've started a whole new Homecoming tradition," I said. "Go, Petal Pushers!" I turned to Nicholas. "Thank you," I said simply.

"My pleasure," he returned, with a grin.

"Thank you both!" Mom said. "I'm headed over to find everyone. You coming?" I checked my watch. We still had time before the parade.

"Treat you to a hot chocolate?" I asked Nicholas.

"I thought you'd never ask!" he said.

"All right, see you later," said Mom.

Nicholas and I strolled over to the concession stand that was on the quad and got in line.

"Well, hello there, Delphinium," said a snotty voice from behind me.

I took a deep breath and turned around. It was Ashley, of course, in leather leggings and a long, fuzzy-looking, off-white sweater coat. I sighed. My jeans with the hole in the knee, McIlhenny sweatshirt, and one red, one yellow high-top now seemed completely kiddish, as Pops would say.

"Hi, Ashley," I said with a sigh, just wanting to get my hot cocoa and be on my way.

Nicholas leaned forward. "Hi, I'm Nicholas," he said. Ashley looked him up and down.

"Oh *you're* Nicholas," she said and nodded. She turned back to me.

She bit her lip. "Del, I've been meaning to tell you. What you said at school the other day really hit close to home," she said.

I narrowed my eyes at her. "What are you talking about?" I asked.

"I *was* being friends with your sister to get to you," she said.

"I thought so," I said. But why was she admitting it to me?

"But not for the reason you think," she said. She gulped. "Not to be mean. I did it because . . . because . . . I miss being friends with you," she finished softly.

Wait — had I heard her correctly? "*You* miss *me*?" I said.

"I do. Being friends with Rose kind of helped. A bit."

I took a deep breath. This was completely unexpected.

Could it really be true? "Oh, Ashley," I said. "I didn't realize . . ."

Ashley barked out a laugh. "Well, I guess I'm not such a bad actress after all!" she said.

I glared at her. "Like I really believed you!" I snapped.

"Oh, I don't know about that," said Ashley with a smirk. "You seemed pretty convinced!"

I was so flustered I stepped away from her, bumping right into the person ahead of me in line.

"Actually," said Nicholas, looking from me to Ashley, "I've read quite a bit about body language, and I'm about ninety percent sure that Ashley was telling the truth. She really *does* miss your friendship, Del."

"That is so not true!" Ashley spluttered. "At all!" She stormed off angrily.

I turned to Nicholas. "Really?" I asked him.

Nicholas laughed. "No! I don't know the slightest thing about body language," he said. "I just made it up."

I grinned at him. "Thanks, Nicholas," I said.

"You're welcome," he replied.

I looked at him. "Hey — you want to hang out with me at the game?" I asked. I was seeing him in a different light. Nicholas was smart. And talented. And, I grudgingly admitted, now that he had grown into his big ears, maybe even a little bit cute. I'd never be interested in him in that way, of course — he was more like a brother. Or a slightly annoying cousin. But I was pretty sure that we could be friends.

Nicholas shook his head. "I've kind of got a date for the game," he said with a grin. "With Sabrina. And then afterward we're going to head over to the library. Can you believe she's never seen the original Tupperware exhibit?"

I shook my head. "I can't," I said.

"I'm supposed to meet her right here on the quad," he said. "You want to wait with me?"

"Sure," I said. I sat down with him on a nearby bench and pulled out my cell phone. I took a deep breath. I was going to text Hamilton.

R U AT HOMECOMING? I typed in. I found his name and pressed SEND.

A moment later, Nicholas pulled out his phone. He flipped it open, and looked at me like I was crazy.

"What?" I said.

"Of *course*, I'm at Homecoming," he said. "Are you losing it?"

"Holy crud," I said. It all made perfect, awful sense. I had mixed up Nicholas's and Hamilton's numbers when I was inputting them! Those irritating messages from Nicholas had actually been nice messages from Hamilton. And what had I called him? Oh that's right. *Einstein!* No wonder he wasn't talking to me!

"I meant to send it to a guy named Hamilton," I explained, not sure whether to laugh or cry. "And now he'll probably never talk to me again."

And then, as if I had summoned him, there was Hamilton, striding across the quad. My heart skipped a beat.

"That's him," I said, pointing.

"What are you waiting for? Go talk to him," said Nicholas.

I took a deep breath. Nicholas gave me a nudge. I stood up and sprinted after him.

When I caught up with him, I touched his arm. "Hey, Hamilton," I said.

He turned around. "Don't you mean Einstein?" he asked. He did not look amused.

"You're never going to believe why that happened," I started to say.

"Try me," said Hamilton.

So, as we stood under a maple tree, red and yellow leaves drifting down around the us, surrounded by people in moose antlers, I told him the whole story. And he burst out laughing.

"I was sort of mad," he said.

"I can only imagine," I told him.

"So does that mean you want to go to the game with me?" he asked.

"Definitely," I said.

The parade was magical. Marching bands, cannons shooting out red-and-yellow confetti, the McIlhenny Moose galloping around, pumping up the crowd. I was pleased to see that lots of people were wearing our corsages. Then what we had all been waiting for: the float with the Homecoming King and Queen and their court.

My heart swelled with pride as I saw Emily, the beautiful Homecoming queen, wearing the amazing dress we had created. People went crazy when they saw it. Someone stepped on my foot as they jostled to get a picture, but I didn't mind. "I've never seen anything like it!" the woman next to me said in wonder.

"Nice dress," Hamilton said.

"I like the bouquets," I said back, even though I thought they were a little boring. And that's all we said to each other about flowers all day.

We met up with Becky, Amy, Heather, and Jessica in the stands. I gave an excited squeal when I saw they were each wearing a corsage. They looked awfully surprised when I showed up with Hamilton. But no one said anything, thank goodness. Becky squeezed my hand and I squeezed back. "I'll explain later," I whispered to her.

We had a great time at the game, doing the wave, chatting away, munching on hot dogs and popcorn as we cheered for the beleaguered Moose. They were massacred as usual. But no one seemed to mind.

In all the fun, I almost forgot that tomorrow was D-Day. *D* as in the biggest decision my family was ever going to make.

Chapter Thirteen

Nicholas shook my hand solemnly. "Thanks for a great time, Del," he said. "I can't believe all the amazing shots I got at the game, and best of all — of the Tupperware."

I giggled. "Well, thank you, Nicholas, for all your help. The corsage idea was brilliant." I was willing to give credit where credit was due.

"Actually, I think that figuring out why the van was missing was even better," he said, opening the car door and sliding into the passenger seat. "I mean, that's how you got the rose dress back in time for the parade, you know. That would have been a disaster."

I leaned in the window. "That was pretty good, too," I told him with a grin.

"Hey, can you tell your friend Sabrina I'll be IMing her as soon as I get home?" he asked me.

"Actually," I said, "why don't you just surprise her?" I didn't have the heart to tell him she was no friend of mine.

"Even better," he said. "Maybe we'll be back for Homecoming next year!"

"That would be great," I said. And surprisingly enough, I meant it.

We all waved as Debbie backed out of the driveway and they took off down the street. Mom dabbed her eyes with an orange bandanna with one hand and waved wildly with the other.

After they were gone, we headed inside in silence. The butterflies in my stomach were out of control. It was time for our family meeting.

The plan was to hear all the evidence and then everyone would vote on what they thought we should do. I knew that Dad and Great-aunt Lily had found an acceptable new location in a strip mall, with plenty of parking. And that when Dad had mentioned the amount that Boston Beans had offered us, the realtor told him we'd be insane not to jump at the offer. It was tradition versus cold, hard reality. I wasn't feeling very positive about how things were going to turn out.

We all filed inside and sat stiffly in the living room as we waited for Aunt Lily to arrive. Mom grabbed my hand and squeezed it. The room felt heavy with tension. "Put that away," Mom barked at Dad as he took out his phone. "Please," she added, putting her hand gently on his arm.

"Why is everyone so cranky?" Poppy wanted to know.

"We're trying to make a big decision," Rose told her.

Poppy shrugged. "Oh. That's a little too boring for me," she said.

Finally, the doorbell rang. Dad got up and ushered Aunt Lily inside. She was dressed even more formally than usual, wearing a black wool coat with a mink collar.

"Hello, everyone," she said stiffly.

"Hello, Aunt Lily," we chorused halfheartedly.

Dad helped Aunt Lily remove her coat. She nodded to us all briskly. With a sigh, Mom stood and we all trudged into Dad's office to place our call to Gran and Gramps.

Dad dialed them up and before we knew it, their faces filled the screen. I was happy to see them, but I missed them so much it hurt. Mom filled Gran and Gramps in on how well Homecoming had gone.

"We may have lost the traditional Homecoming

business this year, but we more than made up for it with new business," she explained. "We ended up making an amazing dress entirely out of roses."

"What?" said Gran. "Entirely out of roses? It must have been spectacular! You made it, Daisy?"

"She did!" I said proudly. "I sent you some pictures. Check your e-mail!"

"I can't wait to see it!" said Gramps. "Now that's thinking!"

"That's not all," Dad said. "We also single-handedly started a Homecoming corsage craze. We made hundreds and we sold every one."

"Sounds like you guys were handed lemons and you made yourselves some lemonade!" said Gramps.

"And some lemon meringue pie, too!" Gran exclaimed.

"Well, there was one disappointing thing," I told them. "The McIlhenny Moose got clobbered as usual."

"Nothing like consistency," said Gramps. His face grew serious. "And now for the hard part. How are you doing with the decision to sell?"

We all looked at each other uneasily. Dad spoke up first. "We found a location that could really do the trick," he said. "It's big, brand-new, has plenty of parking, and is next door to the most popular pharmacy in town. We could buy it with the money that Boston Beans is offering and still have enough money to do a complete remodel on the shop, including a state-of-the-art flower cooler. We could even hire another designer. Even with all that . . ."

"Enough!" said Aunt Lily. We all turned to look at her, our mouths open. She sounded mad. I braced myself for what she was about to say.

"I . . . I . . . I . . . can't do this," she finally said. "I know we could use the money, and Ben, you've put so much work into this, but it just isn't right. Petal Pushers belongs on Fairfield Street."

There was a moment of dead silence.

I stood up, unable to contain myself. "Yay!" I shouted, jumping up and down.

Rose and Aster high-fived each other. It was obvious that Poppy was not exactly sure about what had transpired, but she started jumping up and down, too. Mom wiped her eyes with her bandanna. I stole a glance at my great-aunt, who was rooting around in her pocketbook.

Was mean old Aunt Lily crying, too? I handed her a tissue from the box on the desk.

"Thank you, Delphinium," she said, not making eye contact with me.

"Well, that's a relief," said Gramps.

"Thank you, Lily," Gran said softly.

"I just couldn't let us sell it," Aunt Lily said, staring down at the floor. "Too many memories. Remember the fun we would have playing on the floor at Mom and Dad's feet, making bouquets out of the discarded flowers while they worked?"

Gran laughed. "The parties we used to throw for our dolls! Weddings, birthdays, tea parties . . ."

"I'll never forget the funeral we had for that dead praying mantis we found," Aunt Lily reminded her.

"You made the most beautiful casket spray," Gran reminisced. "Dad was so impressed!"

Aunt Lily laughed. "He was, wasn't he?"

Gran was nodding and dabbing tears from her eyes at the same time. "Lily, did you know that if you look closely at the doorway to the office, you can see the pencil marks from when Mom would measure us?"

"Really?" said Aunt Lily. "I'll have to look next time I'm in the store."

"'All's well that ends well; still the fine's the crown; What'er the course, the end is the renown,'" said Dad. "That's . . ."

"Shakespeare," we all finished for him.

"That's right!" he said. "You guys have been paying attention!"

Aunt Lily cleared her throat. "There's just one thing," she said.

We all looked at her warily. What could it be?

"I'd like to be a little more involved in the store," she told us. "I used to be quite the flower arranger back in the day!"

I stole a glance at Mom. She put on a big (and I'm certain, quite fake) smile. "Of course, Aunt Lily," she said. "That would be lovely."

"Ben, will you do the honors?" Gramps asked.

Dad looked confused.

"Telling Boston Beans to buzz off, of course!" Gramps said.

"With pleasure!" Dad cried.

Gran and Gramps signed off, promising they would be here for Thanksgiving. Then Mom ran into the kitchen and came back with a tray holding a bottle of sparkling cider and some champagne flutes. She popped it open and we had a toast.

"To Petal Pushers!" she said.

"To Petal Pushers!" we echoed. We all clinked glasses.

Then we all hugged and kissed. (Great-aunt Lily looked shocked to get caught up in one of Dad's bear hugs.) When I had drained my glass, I yawned and stretched. It had been an exciting, action-packed weekend. I was really glad things were back to normal. . . .

"Oh no!" Dad yelled in horror. "What have I done?"

I spun around. What was wrong now?

My father was staring at his phone. "My garbanzo beans withered," he said. "Now I'm never going to have enough snozzleberries to buy that tractor!"

Okay, so not *entirely* back to normal. But I grinned anyway. Things not being entirely normal *was* normal for my wacky family.

And I was glad for that.

Petal Pushers

Four sisters. One flower shop.
Will disaster bloom?

Don't miss any of these fresh, sweet reads!

POISON APPLE BOOKS

The Dead End

This Totally Bites!

Miss Fortune

Now You See Me...

Midnight Howl

Her Evil Twin

Curiosity Killed the Cat

At First Bite

THRILLING.

BONE-CHILLIN

THESE BOOKS

HAVE BITE!